silent
confessions

Coming Soon

Deadly Desires

JULIE KENNER

silent
confessions

HARLEQUIN®HQN™

Recycling programs
for this product may
not exist in your area.

ISBN-13: 978-0-373-77926-0

SILENT CONFESSIONS

Printed in U.S.A.

Thanks to the folks in the Detective Bureau, NYPD,
for answering my stream of questions about
procedural details. And thanks to the Austin P.D.
for filling in some gaps, and to Cyndee Duhadaway
for putting me in touch with the right folks. Also,
a big thanks to Mishell Kneeland for not running
far and fast from my unilateral announcement that she'd
become my own personal NYC expert, and for patiently
answering my avalanche of emails. To all of you,
the help provided was invaluable and accurate.
Any embellishments (or mistakes) are purely my own.

chapter
one

Don't be frightened, darling; lovers can say anything. Those words, out of place in colder moments, add fresh relish to the sweet mystery of love? You will soon say them, too, and understand their charm.

Detective Jack Parker snapped on a pair of latex gloves and plucked the note off the satin-covered pillow. Neatly typed on pale pink paper, the writing seemed innocent enough. Hell, in another time, another place, the words could have been romantic, lovers sharing naughty endearments and euphemisms meant only for each other.

Tonight, though, the words had been meant to terrify. *Bastard.*

Their Casanova had struck twice before, and so far the police didn't have one solid lead. The situation ate at his gut.

Jack hated to lose.

Closing his eyes, he counted backward from ten, letting the efficient bustle of the crime-scene investigators wash over him. The gentle *whoosh* of the vacuum collecting telltale fibers, the *click-whir* of the camera documenting the room. New York's finest were on the job. They'd catch the creep.

They had to.

Taking a deep breath, he opened his eyes and saw his partner, Tyler Donovan, waving him over from the doorway. Jack made his way across the sprawling bedroom, passing the note off on the way to be processed with the rest of the evidence.

"Give me some good news."

"Dollar beer all week at Martini's," Donovan said with a shrug. "That's about the best I can do. Here, we got nada."

"Not what I wanted to hear."

"No kidding. All I can tell you is that they don't have a clue who's doing this. But the wife's pretty shook up."

"Can't say I blame her." Over Donovan's shoulder, Jack could see Caroline Crawley sitting unnaturally straight on an upholstered bench in the living room. Her husband, anchorman Carson Crawley, stood stone-faced behind her, his hand resting on her shoulder. Both had the shell-shocked expression of the violated. It was a look Jack knew well. That haunted, injured look had marred his cousin Angela's face many years ago.

With only three months separating them in age and two blocks separating them in distance, he and Angie had been constant companions. At least until the summer of her sixteenth year.

The monster hadn't even waited until after dark. He'd

pulled Angie off her bike right after school as she'd ridden by the local gas station, dragged her into the putrid men's room, and left her there when he was done with her. The gas station owner had found her hours later, unconscious and battered, her beautiful face disfigured and both arms broken. Her face and arms had healed; the rest of her hadn't.

Sweet Angie took her own life exactly one year later.

Jack may have joined the force because he was a third-generation cop. But he'd clawed his way up the ranks to detective in the sex crimes division because it was personal.

Yes, Jack knew the expression on Caroline Crawley's face. Knew it well. And it never failed to spark a rage that wouldn't dim until the perp was dead or behind bars. Until then, nothing else mattered.

"Crawley's shipping the kids off to his parents'," Donovan said, pulling Jack from his memories. "Wants the wife to go, too, but she says no. And they're gonna have the locks changed and the security system upgraded." He shook his head. "How the hell did the bastard get in? We're twenty floors up. This place has more security than Fort Knox."

"I'm more concerned that he wanted in at all." Jack fumbled in his jacket pocket for a cigarette, then remembered he'd quit a year ago. "Our Casanova's turning dangerous."

"No kidding. But it doesn't make sense. For three weeks he's been stuffing their mailbox with nudie postcards and pages ripped out of *Lady Chatterley's Lover*. Then suddenly he decides it's time to sneak into her apartment and leave a little present on her pillow? Why now?"

Donovan was right. It didn't make sense. And the real kick in the pants—the reason Jack had been spending twenty hours a day following dead-end leads—was that they weren't any closer to finding their perp than they'd been three weeks ago.

He clenched his fist, fighting back rage. Damn it all to hell. What were they missing?

"And why Mrs. Crawley?" Donovan added. "We've been over her life with a fine-tooth comb and can't find one person who'd do this to her."

"Then we haven't looked hard enough."

Donovan opened his mouth as if to argue, but shut it quickly enough. After two years as partners, he'd learned when not to argue. Instead he nodded. "Okay. Maybe. But could be it's just random. Carson Crawley's face is all over the six o'clock news. Maybe our guy's just fixated on the celebrity's wife. Could be he's just a weirdo."

"Great. A celebrity stalker who has no fingerprints and leaves no trace." Irritated, Jack ran his fingers through his hair and headed through the open front door and into the plush hallway. The scene was under control, and he thought better when he was walking. "What aren't we seeing?"

"Hell if I know." Donovan jammed the elevator button with his thumb. "But we're not gonna figure it out tonight. It's two in the morning. And I left a very naked, very willing woman in my bed."

"That explains why you look so tired." Since his divorce

nine months ago, Donovan had pretty much joined the babe-of-the-month club.

"Not tired. Refreshed." Donovan grinned. "She's got a sister if you're interested."

The elevator opened and they stepped on. "They've all got sisters. Does your lady have a name?"

"Mindy, Cindy. Something like that."

"You're a sick man, Detective Donovan."

"Not sick. Robust."

Jack flashed his bad-cop scowl, the one he usually reserved for interrogation rooms.

"All right, all right," said Donovan, his hands held up in surrender. "Her name's Cindy, this is date number four, and she really does have a sister."

He followed Jack off the elevator, and they stepped outside. Automatically, Jack reached for his tie and loosened the knot at his throat.

Donovan shoved a hand in his pocket, then pulled out a paperclip. "So how about it?" he asked, twisting the clip. "Let's give her a buzz. Go grab breakfast somewhere."

"Why would I want to go out with a woman so desperate she'd agree to a date at two in the morning?"

"She's a nurse. End of shift. Cindy'll call her, she'll meet us, we'll have a little party."

"No." Maybe the girl wasn't a total loser, but no.

"You gotta take a break from the case sometime, man. It'll still be there in the morning."

Jack flashed Donovan a withering look. "And that pretty much goes to the heart of the problem."

"There's more to life than nailing the bad guys, Jack. You gotta nail some women, too."

Groaning, Jack rolled his eyes. "You are one sick puppy."

"Yeah, but at least I'm out there, not holed up behind a desk licking my wounds."

Jack bristled. "You're treading on thin ice, Donovan."

"I'm just worried about you."

"Nothing to worry about. I'm not licking any wounds. I'm the one who broke it off with Kelly, remember?"

"That's my point. You broke it off with her so you could focus on your career."

True enough. Kelly had wanted three things—a ring, Jack's love and Jack's time. But the truth was, all he was capable of giving her was the first one. Money could buy a ring. But he couldn't manufacture love no matter how hard he tried. And he didn't want to cut back on his job. Not for Kelly. Hell, maybe not for anybody.

"But you're not a monk, man," Donovan said, punctuating his point. "And twenty-hour days are going to kill you. You need to get laid."

"Dr. Donovan's prescription for success?"

"Shit, yeah."

"I can find my own women," Jack said. "I don't need you pimping for me."

Donovan snorted out a laugh. "Too bad. I've got great taste." Donovan stopped alongside his beat-up Jeep, parked in front of a fire hydrant. "Come on. Cindy's sister might be the woman for you. You could be missing out on the lay of a lifetime."

It was Jack's turn to laugh. "I'll risk it," he said. "Right now I just want to go home and get some sleep."

"Sleep?" Donovan asked, doubt lacing his voice.

"That's what I said." And that's exactly what he intended to do. Right after he swung by the precinct and took another look at the file.

The summer heat taunted her, denying her sleep. In front of her, photocopied pages from *The Pearl* and *The Boudoir* were strewn haphazardly across the sturdy oak door she'd converted into a desktop. Ronnie picked up a page at random, needing to work, but not in the mood. Instead of analyzing the words as a proper academic should, Ronnie lost herself in the prose, her pulse quickening as she skimmed the text.

There, on the page, the fictional Monsieur lifted his lover's skirts, revealing her stockings...her garters...her sex. With reverence, he urged her thighs apart, then knelt in front of her, his tongue laving her intimately.

With a low moan, Ronnie closed her eyes, imagining it was her, and not the fictional Bertha, who was the subject of the Monsieur's attentions. Arching her neck, she trailed her fingers down the front of her thin cotton nightshirt. Her body shuddered as she ran her hands over the swell of her breasts, letting her fingers linger on her nipples, which hardened under her touch.

Lord, she was frustrated.

And pitiful.

She pulled her hands away and sat straight in her chair, her elbows on her desk. Across the room, the window air conditioner spit out cool air at random, barely making a dent in the oppressive heat.

What kind of academic got all hot and bothered while trying to study? Well, that was easy. An academic who was stupid enough to pick a research topic related to erotic literature, and then dumb enough to go and read source material way past her bedtime. And *The Boudoir,* no less.

Not that the research wasn't...fascinating. At the rate she was going, she'd need to invest in industrial-strength air-conditioning. As if on cue, the ancient window unit shuddered and gasped, finally belching out one last burst of tepid air before dying completely.

Considering the temperature for the rest of the week was supposed to hit record highs, she probably should have expected massive equipment failure. First the robbery, then two days without even a word from the cops, then the argument with her academic adviser, and now this. The final insult of an already rotten week.

A cold shower, that's what she needed. Surely she'd sleep better if she could just cool down. Frustrated, she took off her glasses, tossing them onto her desk. She rubbed the bridge of her nose, then ran a hand through her sweat-dampened hair. Who was she kidding? Even if her apartment was climate controlled to a constant sixty-eight degrees, she'd still be awake.

Since the robbery, every creak and shudder of the old building made her jump. Especially since the police had been so closemouthed, not letting her know if they had any leads as to who might have broken into her book-store downstairs.

And it had been such a creepy robbery, too. As if someone had just wanted to rifle through her stuff. The store was filled with expensive books and rare manuscripts, and yet none of that was touched. Not any of the near-priceless incunabula in the display case, not the clamshell set of Dickens's serials displayed behind her work desk, not even the three hundred dollars in petty cash she'd left in the top drawer.

Instead, her burglar had left books strewn about on the floor and on top of bookshelves, and had tossed the papers from her desk all over the floor. It had taken Ronnie a full day to sort through and organize her lecture notes, personal correspondence and business bills.

Annoying and creepy. Definitely creepy. Combine the robbery with the looming deadline for her dissertation outline, and she doubted she could sleep even if the place were tomb silent, meat-locker cold and surrounded by armed guards.

A trickle of sweat ran down her temple and she brushed it away, trying to focus on work. Less than twenty-four hours ago, her faculty adviser had rejected her dissertation topic—the Influences of Erotic Literature on Contemporaneous Popular Culture—as too broad, and now she had to come up with a narrower focus, and fast. Since she was wide-awake at 4:00 a.m., the least she could do was spend the time productively. She'd worked hard to build up the store's collection of erotic art and literature, and she'd hoped that combing through some of the volumes would inspire her.

She grimaced, thinking of her body's reaction to the

Monsieur's story. She'd been *inspired,* all right, just not academically. Instead, she was feeling hot, bothered and sorry for herself, comparing her lack of anything remotely resembling a sex life to the baudy, exotic and most definitely *erotic* adventures of the women she spent evening after solitary evening reading about.

Leaning her head back, she sighed. A man. That's what she needed.

No. She pressed her fingers to her lids and rubbed her closed eyes. Between her course work and trying to make the bookstore profitable, she was fully occupied one-hundred-and-twenty percent of the day. And even that wasn't enough.

Besides, she'd had a man, and while the sex had been fabulous, Burt had been anything but. She shook her head, banishing the still-vivid images of her ex-husband and his receptionist, butt-naked, going at it on *her* two-hundred-and-fifty thread-count Ralph Lauren sheets. Not a pretty picture.

At least she was rid of him. She'd marched straight from their apartment to her attorney's office. Good riddance to bad rubbish. Going on two years now. Hell, maybe she'd throw a party.

No, she didn't need a man. But maybe a vibrator…

Nibbling on her lower lip, she toyed with the pages on her desk, papers that revealed passions and emotions that reached powerful heights. Heights she'd been sorely missing lately.

What irony. Veronica Archer—the owner of Archer's Rare Books and Manuscripts, a specialist in rare erotica, author of more than twenty scholarly articles on erotic books and art—had the most pitiful sex life imaginable.

She shoved the thought away. She was happy with her life. Right now, her career came first. It wasn't a sacrifice—it was liberating. While her friends were waiting by the phone wondering if Mr. Right was going to call, she was free to occupy her mind with more interesting pursuits. Unlike Joan, her twenty-four-year-old hot-and-heavily-into-dating assistant, Ronnie could gain a pound without having a panic attack, could rent all the sappy movies she wanted, and could care less about the fine art of small talk.

With a sigh, she gathered the pages and her notes. Since the air-conditioning had conked out, if she wanted to get any reading done tonight, she'd have to do it downstairs. At least the electrician was coming back to the store in the morning. Maybe he could coax the contraption into surviving one more summer.

Her door opened up onto the interior stairs that connected the five floors of the old family brownstone. Formerly for servants' access, the stairs now ran from the bookstore on the first two floors, to the storage room on the third floor, to Ronnie's apartment on the fourth and her brother Nat's on the fifth.

She eased the door open and stepped onto the landing, avoiding the weak spot that always rang out like a shot. Since the burglary, Nat had been fussing over her safety. No sense letting him know she was having trouble sleeping.

On the ground floor she paused and looked back up

the stairs, making sure no light appeared from above. Nothing. Good. She would down a gallon of coffee in the morning and Nat would never know just how lousy she'd been sleeping lately.

Slowly, carefully, she turned the knob, pushing the door at just the right speed to minimize the creak of the old hinge she never remembered to fix. When she'd maneuvered the door open enough to squeeze through, she slipped in, shut the door and flipped on the light.

Success.

"Careful, sis, you might wake me."

Or not.

With a frown, she surveyed the room, finally locating Nat in one of the cushy armchairs she kept near the antique furnace. "What are you doing down here?" she asked.

"I figured you were still a little antsy after our uninvited guest. Thought I'd wait up and commiserate with you."

"I'm not antsy," she lied.

"Come on, Ronnie. I know you too well. Besides, it's not quite morning and you've been awake for hours."

"Hours?" She dropped her papers on the antique desk that served as the command center for the store, then hit the power switch on the coffeemaker she always kept filled and ready to brew. "How do you know how long I've been up?"

He waggled his eyebrows, the familiar gesture making her laugh. "I see all."

"Uh-huh," she said, dropping into the chair opposite him. "Give."

"I got home about one. Your light was on. About an hour ago, I woke up, dead thirsty, and realized I was out of soda." He leaned forward and gave her knee a quick squeeze. "When I came down here to grab one from the break room, what did I see but a light still shining from underneath my darling little sister's front door?"

"Maybe I went to sleep with the lights on," she said, then immediately regretted it. Staying awake or sleeping with the lights on—either way he'd assume she was nervous, scared of the dark, or otherwise put off by the robbery.

On cue, he shrugged and took a swallow of Mountain Dew. "I'm just looking out for you, Ron. I don't like worrying about you. Knowing you're scared."

"Nat," she crooned, trying out her reasonable-and-responsible-sister voice, "you're supposed to be on a plane in just a few days. A Galápagos shoot for *National Geographic* is a really big deal. Worry about *that*. Not me."

"I'll always worry about you, McDonald."

Ronnie rolled her eyes at the silly nickname. During eighth grade, she'd had a crush on Billy Hobbs, who happened to like redheads, not girls with uncooperative, mousy-brown ringlets. After a little mishap with a bottle of hair dye, Ronnie had ended up with curls more flaming orange than sultry red. Billy Hobbs had laughed and Nat had cheered her up. And after he was sure she'd survive, he'd pinned her with the rather annoying nickname of Ronald McDonald. Apparently the rule book for big brothers required an obnoxious-to-nice ratio of about three to one.

She looked at him fondly, and he smiled back, an easy gesture. Finally, she shook her head, half laughing. "You're impossible."

"That's why you love me."

"Who says I do?" she teased.

He flashed her a smirk. "I know all. I see all."

As she laughed, he took another sip of soda. She squinted at the nasty-looking scratch above his elbow. "What did you do?"

"Huh?" He followed her gaze. "Oh, that." He shrugged, dropping his arm. "I was hanging some of my photos and I tripped. Managed to catch my arm on the nail."

"Ouch," she said. She ran her finger along it, and he winced, as if he was holding back a burst of pain. "Jeez, Nat. Is it infected? What did you put on it?"

He tugged his arm away, looking sheepish. "Hydrogen peroxide. It's fine. I'll put some more on it when I go back up."

She frowned but didn't argue. "You shouldn't be doing that, anyway. I told you I wanted to frame your stuff for you, and then hang it. You need more color in your apartment." Her brother was a wonderful photographer, but he kept most of his best stuff shoved in boxes, and he had no decorating sense whatsoever. For more than a year, she'd been promising to place his stuff in colorful frames and arrange it on his deathly dull bare walls. Being a terrible sister, she hadn't yet gotten around to it.

"No big deal," he said. "And no fair trying to change the conversation." He aimed a stern finger in her direction. "I know what you're trying to do."

She rolled her eyes. "I'm *fine*. Really." She spread her arms wide. "Snug as a bug in a rug."

"You're nervous," he said, holding out his hand to her. "I don't like that."

Bless his big-brotherish little heart. She took his hand, giving it a little squeeze. Ever since their mom had walked out, Nat had played parent. Granted, it was a role that needed playing, particularly since her dad had been too busy with his books to take any interest in the job.

Nat's father had died when he was five, and their mother had married Kendall Parker, who'd promptly adopted the little boy. A couple of years later, Ronnie had come along. Two days after Ronnie's fifth birthday, Ashley Parker had decided she was tired of motherhood. She'd walked out and never looked back. Then twelve, Nat had been Ronnie's calm during the storm of the next few years. He'd helped her through a typically rocky adolescence, and held her hand when her father had died.

But she was thirty years old now, and Nat's days as the daddy du jour had run their course.

But when she told him so, he just shook his head. "I don't care how old you are, Ron. You're still my little sister and I'm gonna watch out for you."

Exasperated, she pulled away. "I don't need looking out for. It was just a robbery. The electrician is coming tomorrow to rewire the alarm system."

Nat pressed his soda can against his forehead. *"Ka-ching,"* he said. "The place is a money pit, Ron."

She crossed her arms over her chest. "Then *you* fix it."

He shook his head. "Beyond my capabilities, I think."

She doubted it. Her brother was as handy as they came. He'd built a state-of-the-art darkroom in his apartment, installing the special lighting and other fixtures. But he was also a bit lazy. With the proper motivation, he could do anything. Without it, nothing would ever get done.

She loved him, but the truth was the truth.

"Come on, Ron. We're sitting on a fucking fortune here. Sell the store, sell the building, and we can run off to Paris. I'll take pictures and you can work on your dissertation."

"Nat, we've had this conversation. I'm not selling." She crossed her arms, hoping she looked dug in. They'd been down this road before. They sure as hell weren't going to travel it in the middle of the night. Too many bumps, and Ronnie couldn't afford to stumble.

His chest rose and fell. "Fine. Whatever. I mean, hey, I've got a fabulous apartment in Gramercy Park that I don't have to pay a dime for. It's not like I'm complaining." He met her gaze, his brown eyes dark and serious. "But when my sister stays up all night worrying, I start wondering if maybe she needs a change of scenery."

"I'm not worrying," Ronnie said. "I was working." A half truth. She *had* been working, but only because she was too keyed up to sleep. "Besides," she added, hoping to appease her brother, "the cops are on it. There's nothing to worry about."

He kicked back, feet on the desk. "The cops made any progress?"

She had no idea. "Tons. They've got a zillion leads." Maybe the cops just thought it was a nothing case, and that's why they hadn't updated her. Certainly nothing much was taken. Of course, it was that very fact that gave her goose pimples.

"Ronnie," he said, and she snapped to attention.

"What?"

"What kinds of leads?"

"Oh. I don't know. Just leads." She examined her fingernails.

"For God's sake, Ron. We live here. We have a right to know what they've found out."

She shrugged, wishing she had something definitive to tell him. Hell, wishing she'd actually spoken with an officer. "You know how vague cops can be."

"I know how vague my sister can be."

Ronnie sighed. She knew when she was beaten. "Okay. Fine. I want you on that plane. Short of hiring a guy named Guido, what do I have to do to make sure it happens?"

A slow, smug grin spread across his face. "Well, little sister, I guess you're going to have to hire the biggest, baddest security dude you can find to sit down here at night—"

"I don't think so."

"—or you're going to have to turn on the charm for the cops, and sweet-talk some information out of them."

chapter
two

"Working early or staying late?"

The voice, more or less familiar, filtered through the mush in Jack's brain, finally spurring one cohesive thought—Irving. The voice belonged to Lieutenant Irving. With a grunt, he peeled his face off the government-issue desk and squinted up at his interrogator. "What?" he croaked. Not exactly a stunning response, but it was the best he could manage.

Dan Irving smirked and plopped down a coffee cup. "You need this more than me." He shook a bag. "The doughnuts I'm keeping. Gotta promote those stereotypes."

Jack took a slug of liquid heaven, closed his eyes and let the legal stimulant do its number on his brain. "Fire, I understand. What I don't get is how man survived before caffeine."

"You call this surviving?" Irving swept his arm to encompass the office. "The animals in Central Park got better digs than we do."

Jack grinned and lifted his coffee cup. "But we got a much better menu."

The lieutenant flipped a wooden chair around, straddled it, and Jack pushed a photocopy of Mrs. Crawley's pillow greeting his way. "What do you make of that?"

Irving picked up the copy, held it farther and then even farther away as though he were doing a little trombone number, then ended up holding it at arm's length. Jack bit back a chuckle. The lieutenant refused to give in and buy reading glasses, but if his eyes kept going south, he was going to need longer arms.

"Don't be frightened, darling." Irving frowned. "A threat. But there's something else. Something about the language. It's stilted."

"That's what I think, too."

"The Crawley case?"

Jack nodded. "Third incident. This one, the perp actually got into their bedroom. Needless to say, Mr. and Mrs. Crawley aren't too happy." He took the paper back, frowning at the neatly typed words. "It's…odd. Our perp seems to be quoting something, and it might be important."

"So figure out what he's quoting."

"Already on it." Jack grinned. "Or rather, Donovan is."

Irving chuckled. "What are you up to, Parker?"

"Just doing my job. I called my partner about six-thirty this morning. Said I needed him to track us down a literature professor."

"Don't suppose Donovan's girl of the week took that too well."

"Don't guess she did." Jack stifled a smile, remembering the girl's clear annoyance when she'd answered the phone. He grinned. "Well, if you can't stand the hours, don't date a cop."

Considering Jack had spent the entire night buried under boxes of evidence, while Donovan had spent the night under—or on top of—something much more entertaining, Jack couldn't feel too guilty about the wake-up call. And the fact was, he really did need to find someone who could source that quote—assuming it really was a quote. In the absence of any physical evidence, it was the best lead they had. Hell, it was the only lead.

"So how'd you pull this assignment?" Irving asked. "Sex crimes division going after scraps of paper now?"

Jack shook his head. "Our perp's got a thing for erotica. Book passages and some pretty graphic nudie postcards."

Irving pulled out a doughnut, then passed the bag to Jack before standing. "Pass a nudie postcard my way and we'll call it even."

Jack laughed, and when his stomach growled he realized he hadn't eaten since yesterday's lunch. He grabbed an apple fritter and devoured half of it before Irving crossed the squad room.

Jack was wiping crumbs off his desk when Donovan appeared and dropped into the chair Irving had abandoned.

"You realize you owe me one," Donovan said.

Jack nodded. "Story of my life. Find anyone?"

Donovan shifted smoothly into professional mode. "A

tenured professor of world literature. No summer classes. Family was in the book business for years. Should be in to see you around nine."

"Good. I've got to be in court on the Bleeker case at eleven, so that's perfect."

"I live to serve." Donovan leaned back, his arms crossed over his chest. "Don't forget the vest," he added.

"Wouldn't dream of it," Jack said. The Bleeker matter had taken a nasty turn, child pornography, mob connections, all sorts of shit. And the word on the street was that Darian Bleeker intended to simply get rid of the witnesses. Kevlar had become de rigueur for the fashionable detective. Jack hated the vest, but he sucked it up and wore it on the days he was testifying. The damn thing was miserable in the summer heat, but certainly preferable to getting blown away.

Donovan helped himself to a corner of Jack's fritter. "So I'm guessing you were here all night. Come up with anything else?"

"Nothing definitive."

"Fingerprints?"

"Lab says no."

"What about the paper?"

Jack shook his head, the lack of any serious leads eating at his gut. "Doubtful. Looks to be pretty common notepaper. But this..." He slid the photocopy across the desk again. "See anything odd?"

Donovan shrugged. "Should I?"

"The e rises a bit. One of the forensic guys noticed."

"A typewriter? What? Our perp's not computer literate?"

"Could be a lead—but only if we track down the match."

Donovan grimaced. "Great. Thousands of typewriters in the greater Manhattan area. I'll start combing junk shops," he scoffed.

"I'm hoping your professor can give us some more concrete help," Jack said.

"I guess you are." Donovan looked at his watch. "In the meantime, I'll go to the lab and see if anyone's hobby is typewriters."

Jack downed some coffee. "Have fun."

As Donovan headed off, Jack pulled out the evidence he'd been reviewing all night—the pillow note, two pages ripped from *Lady Chatterley's Lover,* a postcard of a half-naked woman, and three postcards showing men and women in positions that, if the right woman came along, Jack might be tempted to try.

"I was hoping to talk to him now. I'm in kind of a hurry." At the distinctly female voice, Jack looked up, automatically covering the risqué postcards with a manila folder. Near the main doors, a tall woman with a mass of deep brown curls and lips to die for was having an animated conversation with the officer on duty. She looked at her watch, frowned and turned back to the officer. "I'd like to be back at the bookstore by ten."

Bookstore. Thank God she'd arrived early. He had a ton of questions. Jack jumped to his feet and half ran to the front of the room, stopping across the counter from her and sticking out his hand.

"Detective Parker. I think you're here to see me."

Carla, the officer on duty, raised an eyebrow, but he waved her down. The woman shifted her purse and took his hand, sending an unexpected jolt of electricity dancing across his fingertips.

"Veronica Archer." She glanced from Carla to him and back again. Her eyes widened behind the wire frames of her glasses and she held his gaze for the briefest moment before she looked away, color rising on her cheeks. "I...I'm supposed to talk to you?"

"That's right," he said, thankful for small favors. He opened the gate and ushered her through, appreciating the way her hips moved under the clingy knit skirt.

For a brief moment he wondered if Donovan had deliberately picked the sexiest professor on campus to entice him, then dismissed the idea. Off duty, his partner might throw women at him. On the job, Donovan was the consummate professional. Which meant this woman knew her stuff. "I overheard you say that you were in a hurry. Detective Donovan's down at the lab right now."

"Oh." Her easy smile affected him in ways that were hardly professional. With effort, he forced himself to concentrate on her words. "In that case," she added, "thank you for taking the time to talk with me."

Her smile broadened, and he found himself returning it. He cleared his throat. "Right. Well, Donovan and I work together." Jack gestured to a chair, then sat behind his desk. He was grateful for the chair beneath him. As it was, his own knees felt weak. As if this woman had managed to push all his buttons with nothing more elaborate than a glance.

"I see." She crossed her legs, and he forcibly pulled his eyes away. "Is he the one I spoke to before? I didn't remember his name."

"That's right."

She shifted in her seat, her sweater pulling against the swell of her breasts. Jack's mouth went dry.

"Well," she said, "as I mentioned on the phone this morning, what I would like is—"

"Ms. Archer, I should probably just jump in with the information we need from you." The approach seemed prudent. Not only did he need the information, he needed to regain the sense of control he'd lost the second he'd laid eyes on Veronica Archer. "At this stage of the game, we want to keep as much confidential as possible. I'm sure you understand."

Her teeth grazed her lower lip and her brow furrowed. "Well, yes, of course." She frowned, then shook her head. "No. Actually, the truth is I don't. I only want—"

"Please." He pulled out an evidence bag holding a single page and passed it to her, fighting the urge to explain the entire case. Clearly, he was losing it. Not only did his fingers itch to touch her, but something about the woman made him want to open up, to tell her about everything— the anonymous letters and postcards, the frustration of not being able to get a break in the case.

Get a grip, Jack. He was probably just feeling awkward about foisting erotic literature on a woman. Not the kind of activity he tended to imagine in a professional setting. Hell, not the kind of activity he'd ever imagined at all.

Though with Veronica Archer, he could imagine some interesting study-hall activity.

With a mental jerk, he yanked his mind back, annoyed that the mere proximity to a beautiful woman was driving him to distraction. Maybe Donovan was right. Maybe he'd been too long without a date.

"So?" She waved the bag, then dropped it on his table. "Do you recognize it?"

"Sure. D. H. Lawrence. *Lady Chatterley's Lover.*" She looked him straight in the eye, and he thought he saw anger brewing. An unwelcome change from earlier, and one he didn't understand.

"Anything else?" he asked.

"Is this really necessary?"

A hard edge definitely laced her voice, but he supposed that was understandable. She was an academic, probably not used to being second-guessed. But he needed to be sure she knew her stuff. "Yes. I think it is."

"Chapter ten," she said, her voice tight. "Connie and the gameskeeper. They've never been together, really don't even know each other, but he tells her to lie down, and she does, and then he touches her...*that way.*"

She raised an eyebrow and Jack swallowed, feeling a little like a student who'd just failed a test.

"Why do you ask?" she said.

He avoided the question, instead passing her one postcard and then another, each of which she identified without even missing a beat. The lady knew her stuff. Donovan had certainly tracked down the best professor for the job.

But the cards were chump change. Even he and Donovan had eventually discovered the source of the pages and the artwork. Now it was time for the real test. He pushed the photocopy of the pillow note toward her. "What about this? Do you recognize it?"

"Detective…" She paused, frowning, then glanced first at his desktop and then at him. After a moment, she seemed to come to a decision. "I've tried my best to be polite, to be on my best behavior. But I'm not exactly in the mood for pop quizzes, okay?" She tucked her purse under her arm and pushed her chair back, glaring at him, her eyes cold, entirely lacking their earlier warmth. "Yes, my specialty's erotica. But I don't see why I have to play *Jeopardy!* simply to get the police department to do its job."

Jack could practically feel the anger sparking off her like static electricity. He didn't have a clue as to what had set her off, but he had an overwhelming urge to fix it. To make whatever was bothering her better. "Look, Ms. Archer, if there's been some sort of misunderstanding—"

"Misunderstanding? Ignoring my case? Not returning my calls?" She waved a hand at the evidence he'd just shown her. "And now this…this…*attitude* about the fact that I study erotica." She glared at him, green eyes flashing. "It just so happens that I have a significant number of rare books and manuscripts in that store, not to mention the fact that I live above it."

She pulled her cardigan closed, the thin knit stretching tight against her breasts. He shouldn't be noticing, but he couldn't help it any more than he could help his body's reaction. He tried not to stare. Getting caught ogling her at this particular moment probably wouldn't win him any brownie points.

She swallowed. "I'm scared, Detective. Okay? And I don't appreciate being taunted about my profession."

Blinking furiously, she stood up. "I'll call again later for answers," she said. "And I suggest you have some if you don't want me to speak to your supervisor." With a defiant tilt of her chin, she turned and rushed out, heels clicking on the battered linoleum floor.

Jack was as confused as he'd ever been, and she was out the door and gone by the time his brain defrosted. Gears turned in his head, and coherent thoughts started to form from the random words she'd thrown out—*her case, ignoring, scared, answers*. With a groan, he let his head fall onto the metal desktop.

Veronica Archer wasn't a professor, she was a victim.

Way to go, Jack. Arrest the perps and alienate the victims. Smooth move.

And she wasn't just any victim, but one who owned a bookstore and specialized in erotic literature. Except for the problem that he'd managed to completely piss her off, she could probably help him with the Crawley case more than some generic lit professor from the halls of academia. Not to mention the fact that he just plain wanted to see her again.

Glancing up, he noticed a rumpled man in a seersucker suit talking with Carla. The literature professor, he presumed. An image of chestnut curls, emerald eyes and a kissable mouth flashed in his mind. Features held together by a fiery personality he wouldn't at all mind working with.

Instead, he got Professor Nerdsly.

"Detective Parker," Carla called, "this gentleman is here to see you."

Jack waved, letting her know he'd be right there.

"Oh, and Jack? That woman, she said to tell you it came from *The Boudoir.*"

"That was fast." Joan looked up from the computer as Ronnie stalked into the store, the little bell announcing her arrival. She held up a box. "This came for you. From your secret admirer, I'm guessing."

Ronnie half smiled as she took the box, her hideous mood lifting just a little. She pulled the top off to reveal a package of Hershey's Kisses, with a little note in stenciled calligraphy— *Sweets for the sweet.*

Joan looked over her shoulder. "Aw. How sweet," she said drolly. "I say there's gotta be something wrong with him if he won't show his face."

"Don't be mean," she said to Joan. "Whoever's sending them is probably just shy." For about two months now, she'd been receiving anonymous little gifts every week or so. Each contained a message, a bit clichéd, but nice.

She looked more closely at the box. "Mail?"

"Nope. It was sitting outside the door. One of the customers brought it in."

With a shake of her head, Ronnie sighed, wondering if she'd ever figure out who her admirer was. Her guess was Tommy, the shy young man who'd attended each and every one of the free lectures on erotica the store sponsored on alternate weeks.

If that was the case, though, Ronnie almost hoped he stayed anonymous. Tommy seemed like a sweet kid, in a college freshman kind of way, but certainly not her type.

An image of Detective Parker popped into her mind. Speaking of her type…

Joan plucked the box from her hand and grabbed a Kiss. "So what happened? I didn't think you'd make it back before we opened."

Ronnie's foul mood returned as she flung her satchel onto the desk and aimed herself toward the coffee. "It was a totally wasted trip," she said. "They're impossible. *He's* impossible."

"He?" Joan peered at her over the rims of her psychedelic half glasses, apparently this week's venture into nouveau fashion. "He, who?"

Ronnie took a swig of coffee and shook her head as she swallowed. "A detective *he,*" she said, glaring at the turn-of-the-century French postcards Joan was cataloging, the kind of postcards he'd taunted her with at the station.

Waving a hand toward the scattered ephemera, she scowled. "A him with a complex about *that.*"

"No way. Really? That's why nothing's happening with your break-in? The police are prudes?"

Ronnie sipped her coffee. "Looks that way." She sure as hell couldn't think of any other explanation for his odd behavior.

Distracted, she paced in front of the window, watching her neighbors glide by on the way to work. Bank tellers, bus drivers, schoolteachers, stockbrokers. It was an eclectic neighborhood, and she loved it. The familiar sights and smells had comforted her for years. Mrs. Carmichael opening the corner store. Duncan Tanner selling hotdogs from a cart, the pungent smell of sauerkraut filling the morning air.

She'd managed to quell some of her irritation—no, dammit, her *fury*—as she'd walked back from the police station. But now that anger was rallying, slamming through her stomach with even more force than before. Someone had violated her sanctuary. This neighborhood. Her *life*. How *dare* the cops soft-pedal her robbery just because she dealt in erotic literature.

And the fact that Detective Parker was so damn good-looking only added to her annoyance. For reasons she wasn't inclined to examine too closely, he'd been on her mind during the entire walk back from the station, the echo of his touch still lingering on her fingers.

A particularly annoying fact, considering that Detective Parker had been a total jerk. Probably one of those macho holier-than-thou guys who thought a woman should be prim, proper and submissive. Heaven forbid a woman take the initiative where sex was concerned.

Of course, her extensive reading didn't count as the real thing. She grinned. For that matter, neither did a vibrator. *He could scratch that itch....*

The decadent thought slammed through her, and her knees went weak. She grabbed the side of a bookshelf for support as her mind filled with an image of piercing gray eyes and an angular jaw dusted with a shadow well past five o'clock.

Now, there was a vision that could inspire long nights of study.

Sighing, she sank into the soft leather armchair by the desk, the warm mug clasped in both hands. Despite how much the man had irritated her, her body still tingled at the thought of his touch. She told herself it wasn't him, it was her—oversexed and undersatisfied. But, oh, what a fantasy to imagine Detective Parker doing the satisfying.

She dwelled on the thought a little longer than she should, trying to imagine his hands on her breasts, her waist, her hips. His handshake had been firm, his hands large, and the thought of those hands roaming her body sent little shivers up her spine. It was a fantasy she itched to make reality, but she knew that wasn't possible.

With a sigh, she pushed the daydream away and glanced toward Joan. "So why is it that the handsomest men are inevitably Neanderthals?"

Joan laughed. "One of those, huh? Too bad. We could've used some eye candy around here. A rugged detective doing all that...detecting." She winked. "Could've been fun." She ran a hand through her tousled curls. "I wonder if he likes blondes? Trey's starting to bore me to tears."

"All men like blondes," Ronnie said. "It's carried on the Y chromosome, I think. You have nothing to worry about." She leaned forward, eyes narrowed. "I thought his name was Andy."

"Andy's old news. He stiffed a waitress. I dumped him.

Trey's an artist, very chic, but seriously lacking in the conversation department."

Ronnie rolled her eyes. An artist. Well, that explained Joan's new, get-down-get-funky glasses.

"I bet a detective would have plenty to talk about," Joan added thoughtfully.

"Well, you're just going to have to make due, because there's not going to be any detective-gazing around here." Considering how badly the meeting at the precinct went, that appeared to be an unfortunate reality. "I get the impression we're on our own. I don't think the police are coming at all."

"Who's not coming?" a voice cut in.

Nat. Damn.

Ronnie stood and turned toward the stairwell. He wore jeans and a ratty T-shirt, but his feet were bare. His hair stuck out in a million directions and he looked sixteen instead of more than twice that.

"You look like the dead," she said, hoping the insult would derail the subject.

"Thanks. Who's not coming? The cops?"

"Don't be silly," she said, willing a lie to her tongue as she crossed her fingers in her pocket. "I was talking about the electrician." She shrugged. "Everything's under control."

He shot her a look of pure disbelief before venturing to the coffeepot, filling a cup, then heading back to the stairwell, squeezing her shoulder lightly as he passed by. He paused, looking back at her. "You went like that?"

Automatically, she looked down at her outfit. Skirt, sweater, shoes. Nothing missing or revealing. "Yeah. So?"

He shrugged. "I was just thinking about the kind of guys who hang around police stations. That skirt doesn't leave much to the imagination."

Ronnie crossed her arms over her chest. Nat had been lecturing her on her wardrobe since she was twelve and bought her first training bra. She might be used to it, but it still annoyed her. "It's a knit skirt. It's supposed to cling. And they're called thighs. Everyone has them. I assure you I haven't committed some mighty sin by wearing material that clings." She knew she sounded snappish, but she really wasn't in the mood.

Nat scowled but didn't say anything else. After a second, he changed the subject. "Well, you weren't there very long. What *exactly* did the cops say?"

"Nothing much." She shrugged, swallowing a bit of guilt at the white lie. She'd wasted many a college hour planted in front of television, but not one episode of *Law & Order* sprang to mind. "I guess police departments are pretty busy in the morning," she added, mentally cringing at how lame she sounded. "But a detective is coming by later to give me the full scoop."

Nat rubbed his chin but didn't question her, and she held her breath. Then, with a quick nod and a murmured "okay," he stepped back into the stairwell and pulled the door closed behind him.

The guilt returned. Nat had always been someone she could depend on, rely on, go to with her problems and share her dreams. She truly hated lying to him, but she didn't want him worrying. He had a great opportunity in that job, and she didn't want to see him blow it because of some misplaced worry about his little sister.

She comforted herself with the fact that it wasn't a huge lie. If she worked the phones right and complained loudly enough, maybe she *could* get a detective to come over and give her an update by that evening.

Unfortunately, it just wouldn't be Detective Parker.

chapter
three

The image filtered through his exhausted mind, taunting and teasing him.

Her chestnut hair was pulled back with a single ribbon, the only adornment she wore. In front of her, she held a thin blue scarf. Too sheer for modesty, the material did nothing to hide the dark circles of her nipples. She was smiling, a silent, seductive invitation....

"Jack? Yo! *Parker.* You wanna join the living, buddy?"

With a lurch, Jack pulled himself away from the dream and back to reality, rubbing his hands over his face to try to wake up.

Donovan grinned, glancing down at the desktop. "Fantasizing about the evidence?"

"What?" Jack asked, still groggy. Following Donovan's gaze he saw the postcard. A blonde, nude from the waist up, was flirting with the camera from behind a single flimsy scarf.

Jack blinked. In his dream, the half-naked woman on the old-time postcard had been a brunette. Soft waves cascading over bare shoulders…dancing green eyes…a pert mouth.

Veronica Archer.

Damn, but the woman had gotten to him. He wanted her with an urgency he'd never felt before. And from what he could tell, she was pissed as hell at him.

Too bad.

"There's more," Donovan said, his voice hinting that more didn't mean good.

One last shake of his head and Jack grounded himself. "Tell me."

"Another postcard." He tossed the evidence bag onto the desk. The antique card showed a flapper, this one wearing nothing but stockings, a long strand of pearls and a come-hither smile. "Special delivery just this morning."

Automatically, Jack's eyes drifted to the caged clock on the far wall. Not even ten. "It didn't come by mail."

"Special *pillow* delivery."

Jack frowned. "Shit. Another one."

"Yup. In Brooklyn. A buddy of mine hooked me up with the detective on the case. Seems there's a woman over there who's been getting the same treatment as Mrs. Crawley."

"Great. A serial stalker. Our Mr. Naughty's just spreading cheer all over the boroughs." He sighed. "A blessing for us, a curse for these women."

"Only a blessing if we can find a link between our Brooklynite and Mrs. Crawley."

"Found anything so far?" Jack asked, sure the answer would be no.

"Other than the erotica? Nothing I've discovered in the last forty-five minutes."

Running a hand through his hair, Jack sighed. "Well, it's a solid lead. Let's get on it, start checking their backgrounds. Maybe something will overlap."

"Overlap we've already got."

Nudie postcards and titillating tales. "True enough. This erotica stuff is the key. But damned if I know how."

"What did Professor Baker have to say?" Donovan kicked his feet up onto Jack's desk and twisted the top off a bottle of antacid.

"The man was useless." And tedious. The professor talked like a living telegram, except the *stop* came between every single word, slowing his speech to a mind-numbing pace. After about two sentences, Jack had been ready to strangle the man. "He didn't know a thing about erotica other than that it existed. Oh, and he'd heard of *Fanny Hill*."

Donovan shrugged. "That's something."

"That's nothing. Every junior high school boy looking for a thrill knows about *Fanny Hill*."

The corner of Donovan's mouth twitched. "Not me. I was a *Playboy* kinda guy."

He ignored the comment. "The point is, he's no help. While you're running down connections between the women, I need to find someone who can make sense of this stuff, tell me if there's some pattern, some hidden meaning. Something. *Anything*."

"The department doesn't have that many intellectuals lined up to consult, Jack. You tell the professor to take a hike, and we're gonna be out of luck."

Maybe. Maybe not.

An adorably crooked smile. Emerald eyes. Deep, rich hair. The images swirled in his head, and he mentally reached out, wanting to pull the vision closer.

"Donovan, my man. This just might be my lucky day."

"What do you think?" Joan paced in front of the break-room table, twirling a pencil in her fingers. Postcards, books, prints and sketches littered the tabletop, along with a single three-ring binder, one burst of modernism in a sea of vintage paper.

Ronnie picked up the binder and studied the pages of inventory. "Postwar erotica? Anaïs Nin and Henry Miller? Frank Harris's *My Life and Loves*?"

"Sure. Along with Rojan's lithographs and those cool postcards you brought back from Paris. I bet it'll be our best catalog yet."

"Sort of a banned-books theme," Ronnie said, smiling. Archer's Rare Books issued two catalogs a year covering the finer items from the entire stock, along with one specialty catalog that focused on erotica. Debating with Joan over the theme of the special issue was one of her favorite summer activities.

"They weren't all banned. And, anyway, back in the twenties and thirties, these books really pushed the envelope. It was a whole new era."

With a quick twist, Ronnie pulled her hair up, securing

it with a pencil. "So you're wanting to make some sort of historical or sociological statement?" She frowned. Joan wasn't usually the political type.

"Nah," Joan said with a shrug. "Mostly it's just that we have enough stock from the period to put together a good catalog."

Ronnie laughed. How could she argue with logic like that? Especially since Joan was absolutely right—they could put together a hell of a catalog. Smiling, she nodded. "It's a great idea."

Joan clapped her hands, bouncing like a little girl. "Good. Because I've already started pulling stock. We have Henry Miller, and all four volumes of the Harris— those should fetch a lot—and we have an *inscribed* Anaïs Nin." She did a fake swoon. "I don't know how you get your hands on some of this stuff."

"Trade secret," Ronnie said with a wink. The truth was, it had taken her five years and endless hours building up the store's erotica section. And now that the store had a reputation, collectors often came to her when they wanted to sell a prized book or manuscript.

For as long as she could remember, she'd put her heart and soul into the store, and Ronnie couldn't even imagine another career. With the sad state of the current economy, though, the store was going through some tough times, and Ronnie was doing her damnedest to keep the place profitable. Which made the fact that some creep had broken in all the more infuriating. What if he'd made off with some of her valuable stock?

"What's wrong?" Joan asked, her brow furrowed.

"Nothing. Just thinking about our intruder." She waved her hand, then rifled through the pages in the binder, trying to look nonchalant despite the image of Nat in big-brother mode dancing through her mind. Without an update from the police, he was going to stay in New York instead of taking the career opportunity of a lifetime.

The bummer of it was, so far she'd completely struck out in the detective department. First she'd been scorned that morning by a detective who doubled as her own personal fantasy man, then she'd received the big brush-off when she'd called a few hours later. Detective Parker may have specifically told her that someone named Donovan was on her case, but the police department didn't seem to be too clued in. When she'd complained to the clerk, she'd been told that Donovan wasn't assigned to the matter. So far, she'd left two voice-mail messages for the cop who was supposedly running the show, but she hadn't heard back. She tapped her fingers on the tabletop. "No surprise there," she said.

"What on earth are you talking about?" Joan asked, studying Ronnie over her psychedelic rims.

"Nothing. Ignore me." She shot a glance toward the phone on the wall. "I'll try the precinct again in an hour or so. Sooner or later they'll send someone out just to shut me up."

"Just call 911," Joan said, pulling open the fridge and grabbing a soda. She popped the top and took a swallow. "Tell them we've got another intruder."

Except for the fact that a false emergency call was probably a felony, it sounded like a heck of a plan. This was sort of an emergency, wasn't it? After all, getting rid of Nat really was reaching critical status. So maybe she should…

No. She was a responsible business owner. She paid taxes. She shopped for groceries and voted when she remembered.

But she did *not* make fake emergency calls.

She took a deep breath. "Let's just work on the catalog. I'll call again in a little while."

Joan nodded and brought over an archival box filled with French postcards from the twenties and thirties. "I thought we could scan these and do an illustrated catalog."

Ronnie pulled out one of the sepia cards, lightly running her finger over the edge. Unlike the ones that often turned up at flea markets or on eBay, these were in pristine condition, their edges clean, the images crisp. Someone—the photographer, probably—had hand-tinted each card. Just a touch to highlight the model's jewelry, the ribbon in her hair, the nightgown pooled at her bare feet. The effect was dreamlike. Sensual.

Joan started pulling cards out of the box and laying them faceup on the table. "They're not quite as erotic as the Rojan lithographs, but that's okay, right?"

Ronnie nodded, pulling her thoughts back to the conversation. True, the lithographs tended to feature couples lost in their own private passions, while the postcards each featured a single woman. But, to Ronnie, the cards were just as alluring.

She plucked one out of the box. A nude woman, wearing nothing but a long strand of beads, reclined on a chaise longue, one arm behind her head, a coy look on her face. A sultry siren tempting the man behind the camera. "These cards have secrets," she said, passing it to Joan. "That's why they're so erotic. It's like we're shar-ing a private moment between the woman and her lover."

"I guess that makes her an exhibitionist and us voy-eurs," Joan said, grinning as she pulled up a chair.

Ronnie laughed. "Maybe it does."

"So," Joan said, leaning in closer, "have you ever done anything like that?"

"Exhibitionism?" Ronnie asked, sure her voice was squeaking. "Not hardly."

"No, no, no." Joan rolled her eyes. "Not for all the world." Her devious smile lit up her entire face. "For just one guy. Burt? Anybody?"

"Have you?" An obvious avoidance tactic, but maybe Joan wouldn't notice.

The bell in the main room jingled, cutting off Joan's response. Instantly, she hopped to her feet, pointing a finger at Ronnie. "You stay. See if you like the other stuff I picked for the catalog. I can handle a customer." Then she slipped out the door. A second later, she was back, peering around the door frame. "And the answer to your question is yes. Andy might have been a jerk out in the real world, but in the bedroom he was blue-ribbon ma-terial." She winked, then disappeared again.

Alone, Ronnie gazed at the image of a 1920s ingenue, coy and flirtatious. The woman was perched on the edge of a padded bench, looking almost ethereal as yards of diaphanous material swirled around her.

What would it be like to be that woman? To feel the caress of her lover's eyes on her, to know that he wanted her, and then to open her arms in silent invitation?

She closed her eyes, her body tightening as she imagined the press of her dream lover's body against hers. His hands in her hair, trailing down her shoulder. She'd conjured the dream man the same night she'd walked out on Burt. Her ex-husband may have known all about sex, but her imaginary lover knew all about *her*.

A composite of the men she read about in her books, today he had the face of a certain sexy detective. Her dream lover was a man who wanted to please her, who was so in tune with her—body and soul—that he could almost read her thoughts. A man who knew if she wanted him to kiss her hard and take her right there on the kitchen table, or if she needed it slow and languid. A thousand caresses. Soft words and even lighter touches. Hours of exploration. Teasing and tempting until she couldn't stand it anymore and she begged, *begged*, for him to enter her.

The man in her fantasies played her body like a symphony. Compared to him, Burt had played her like a ukulele.

She wasn't asking for true love. Hell, she wasn't even sure it existed. And the thought of committing to another man...

She shook her head. Right now? No way. But, oh, how she wanted passion. The heart-pounding, blood-boiling, loins-throbbing kind of desire she read about in her books.

She glanced back down at the woman on the card. "I bet you don't have any problem finding lovers," she said.

"Excuse me?"

Oh, hell. That was a male voice, and it most definitely didn't belong to her brother. She felt her face warm, and she looked up…straight into the amused face of Detective Parker.

She swallowed, her cheeks heating in what surely had to be a blush red enough to start a fire. She flashed the postcard for him to see. "I was talking to her," she said, then mentally kicked herself for such an idiotic comment.

"So I gathered."

The corner of his mouth twitched, revealing a sexy dimple, and she cursed herself for noticing. Damn the man for materializing when she had erotica—and him—on the brain.

"I'm not exactly sure what a two-dimensional woman needs with a lover," he added, "but I have no doubts she'll find one." The twitch turned into a full smile and the dimple deepened. "But if you want to help her get lucky, I've got a copy of *Fortune* in my car. Maybe she's into two-dimensional, entrepreneur types."

Swallowing a laugh, she tried to glare at him. "I spent the entire morning being furious with you. Waltzing in here unannounced and making me laugh isn't fair."

Immediately, the smile vanished, replaced by a firm mouth and apologetic eyes. "I'm sorry about earlier," he said, pulling out a chair. He sat opposite her at the table, and she had the unreasonable urge to reach out and touch his hair. "Unfortunately, I'm still not going to be a lot of help."

Still? He hadn't even tried to help earlier. Instead he'd just tormented her.

Even so, something about those pale gray eyes called to her, silently telling her he was sorry, that he did want to help. And that if she kicked him out now, she'd be making the biggest mistake of her life.

Well, maybe that was a little melodramatic, but she did want to hear what he had to say. And, frankly, she hoped it was good. She took a deep breath, then took the plunge. "Okay, give. What are you talking about?"

"Your robbery. No fingerprints, no motive, no suspects. Nothing missing—"

"That I know of."

"Nothing expensive, then. Nothing obvious."

She nodded. "Right."

He shrugged. "That leaves us with nothing to go on."

"You could have just told me that this morning, instead of putting me through the erotica edition of Trivial Pursuit."

"Right." He shifted in his chair, looking distinctly uncomfortable. "Sorry about that."

"You should be." She grabbed up a small Rojan print—the one showing a couple in the back of a limousine, the man in a trench coat, intimately touching his companion, and the woman in a garter and stockings, her skirt around her waist. She waved the print in front of him. "I'm sorry if my life's work offends you, but at least you could be professional, even if this kind of thing rubs you the wrong way."

Coughing, he reached up and tugged at his tie, loosening the knot. His gaze dipped toward the lithograph, then back up to her. His eyes bore into hers with dark intensity, and she shivered, certain he'd touched her without even lifting a finger. "Trust me, lady. That picture rubs me a lot of ways, but *wrong* isn't one of them."

"Oh," she said stupidly. Intelligent thought abandoned her, replaced by the image of her and Detective Parker in the back of a black stretch limo....

Her cheeks heated and she looked away, suddenly fascinated with a brown stain on the ancient vinyl flooring.

He must have picked up on her discomfort, because he took the print from her and turned it facedown on the table. "I didn't mean to offend you earlier. I don't work robberies, and I'm not assigned to your case. I thought you were somebody else." Absently, he picked up the postcard she'd been examining and began tracing the outline with his fingertip.

She waited for him to keep talking, but he stayed silent, apparently waiting to gauge her reaction.

This was all very odd. Part of her wanted to jump out of the chair, chew him out for being a jerk and run back into the main room to help Joan with the customers. Another part of her just wanted to sit and stare into those fabulous eyes.

Besides, she didn't really want to run from him. If what he said was true, he'd actually gone out of his way to help her by investigating her robbery even though it wasn't his case. And she didn't really have any reason to doubt him. After all, the police clerk had told her that neither Parker nor Donovan had anything to do with investigating the robbery. Which left some big questions—who had he mistaken her for, and why was he here?

"Okay, Officer." She took a deep breath. "Keep talking."

"Detective," he said as he laid the postcard faceup on the table between them, like a gambler playing his card. "I need help. With this," he said, glancing down at the card. He looked up again, his eyes burning into her. "I'm assigned to the sex crimes division."

She frowned. "Sex crimes?"

He nodded. "I'm investigating a stalker."

"That stuff you showed me..."

"That's what he's been leaving. His calling cards, you could say."

"I'm not sure I'm following you. How can I help?"

"You're an expert on this stuff, right? Well, I need an education." He smiled, and her heart picked up its tempo. "An erotic education."

Lord have mercy.

The thought that this man, this six-foot-something hunk of pure *maleness* needed help in anything erotic was almost beyond comprehension. The entire situation was surreal. They were sitting in a break room, of all places, surrounded by plastic and Formica, lit with fluorescent lighting. Nothing could be less sensual, and yet every nerve ending in her body was hyperaware. Her pulse beat in her throat, and she was sure her palms were sweating.

"I realize it's not an ordinary request, but I can probably scrounge up some sort of hourly rate. A consulting fee." He shrugged. "Maybe."

She nodded vaguely. He made it all sound so professional, so academic. But academic or not, lessons in erotica with this man would be dangerous…in an absolutely delicious way.

"Miss Archer?"

Nibbling on her lower lip, she glanced down at the card on the table. He was waiting for her answer, waiting for her to put her cards on the table

She picked up the postcard, taking another look at the flapper whose erotic adventures she'd been so envious of only moments before. Then she lifted her eyes to look once again at the man. The shadow of his beard. Those enigmatic eyes. The sturdy angle of his jaw. All of it put together in a face that somehow pushed her senses into overdrive.

If she were thinking rationally, she'd ask more questions, would try to figure out exactly what he needed. After all, she had a business to run and a dissertation to write.

But on the other hand, in a lot of ways he was the answer to her prayers. If she could honestly tell Nat that she had an in with the cops—a source for information about the investigation—surely that would be enough to get him on that plane.

And the work did sound right up her alley.…

But all that was just an excuse, a blatant justification for the real truth—that instinct, primal, pure and dangerous, had taken over. Here was a man who'd made her blood burn since the first moment she saw him, who in five minutes had left her with damp panties and a yearning for more. And that was only after talking business. Just imagine if they'd actually been discussing erotica....

Perhaps she was behaving foolishly, but she wanted to keep him around, even if only for a few more hours.

Slowly, she laid the card back on the table. "It looks like you win, Detective. Class begins promptly at eight."

chapter
four

Jack looked up from the pile of papers on his desk to glance at the clock on the wall.

"It's five minutes later than the last time you looked," Donovan said, hanging up his phone.

"What?"

"The time. Every time I look up you're checking out the damn clock. What? You got a hot date tonight?"

"Unfortunately, it's not a date," Jack said, immediately regretting opening his mouth.

"*Unfortunately?*" Donovan repeated, inflection rising. "What exactly do you have planned for this evening? And does she have a sister?"

Jack laughed. "Mindy cast aside already?"

"Cindy," Donovan corrected him, "and no. Actually things are pretty smooth in Cindy-land."

"I'm shocked. Almost an entire week with the same woman."

Donovan shrugged. "So maybe hell's got a few icicles these days."

"No shit?" Jack knew he sounded incredulous, but his partner had always said he'd settle down with a woman when hell freezes over. If the devil was wearing snow pants, Donovan must have it bad.

Donovan twisted a paper clip as he shuffled a little on his feet. "She's a good gal, you know? And last night, she called me after her shift. Said she felt like hell and could we reschedule. I ended up taking a movie over there and making her some chicken soup and we just sat on the couch. You know, watching the flick." Another shrug. "It was nice."

Jack looked his buddy in the eye. "I'm happy for you," he said.

"Yeah, well, it's always nice to know where your next lay is coming from," Donovan said, but Jack wasn't buying. His partner looked too happy. Too content. Hell, the man was in love. And damned if Jack didn't envy him just a little bit.

Shit.

"So what's this nondate you've got tonight?" Donovan asked.

Jack reached into his desk and pulled out the old catalog Veronica had given him. Homework, she'd called it.

"Archer's Rare Books and Manuscripts." Donovan read the cover. "Winter catalog." He flipped to a random page and his eyebrows shot up before he looked at Jack over the top of the slick pages. "Our nudie postcards."

Jack took the catalog back. "Not ours. But some. According to Miss Archer, the postcards aren't hard to come by. And the one left in Mrs. Crawley's mailbox isn't valuable."

Even though "class" didn't start until that evening, Jack had pressed Veronica for a few answers before he'd left. And he had to admit, the woman knew her stuff.

"So this gal's willing to help us out?"

Jack nodded. "Yup. I'm meeting with her tonight."

"Is she a babe?"

"Excuse me?"

"Just wondering if I should hope your nondate takes on a few twists."

Jack aimed a stern look his partner's way. "If you're looking for something to do…"

"Got plenty," Donovan rushed to say, but he didn't walk away. Jack glared, and Donovan laughed.

"What?" Jack snapped.

"I was right, man. She is a babe. I can see it in your eyes."

Jack scowled but didn't answer. Hell, what could he say? Because the truth was, Veronica Archer *was* a babe. And Jack was counting the hours until his private lesson commenced.

Marina gently lifted the book, tracing her finger over the green-and-white wrapper protected by clear Mylar. After a moment, she sighed. "I wish I could afford it," she said. "But I don't think my bank account could stand the extra strain."

Ronnie sighed, too. At more than five thousand dollars,

the first edition of Henry Miller's *Tropic of Cancer* was one of the few books in stock that garnered a price significant enough to make a dent in her monthly bottom line, and yet not so expensive that it would only sell at auction.

Considering the sorry state of the store's balance sheet at the moment, she'd really hoped the woman would splurge.

Carefully, she replaced the book in the glass case, then twisted the key in the lock. "We also have one copy of the first U.S. edition. It's in excellent condition and it's several thousand less. Would you like to take a look?"

Marina licked her lips, and Ronnie knew she had a sale. The woman was itching to buy something, but had to find that happy medium between a fun splurge and a foolish purchase.

"Well, maybe I could just take a peek," she said, "if it isn't too much trouble." She turned to look behind her, to where the small group of people were milling about near the faux fireplace. "It's tonight's discussion topic, right?"

"That's right," Ronnie said. For about a year now, she'd been conducting minilectures after hours at the store about some of the more accessible famous works of erotica. "But you hardly need a collectible edition to participate. I've got ten paperback copies to share."

"Oh, no," the woman said. "I just meant that you're sure to pique my interest. Last time when you talked about *The Boudoir* and *The Pearl* I went straight to my computer and bought copies of the reissued collections."

This was the third lecture that Ronnie could remember Marina attending, but this was the first time she'd spoken with her. Not unusual. Considering the nature of the talks, Ronnie kept the lectures extremely informal. Folks introduced themselves using only a first name. They could participate or they could hover in the back, listen, then slink out as soon as the lecture was over. Most mingled, but she had a few hoverers, too.

The woman's cheeks tinged slightly with pink. "The thing is, I already have this in paperback. And, well, I've read it a lot. And I'm thinking I'd like something more collectible. Does that make sense?"

"Of course," Ronnie said. "Wait right here and I'll get it for you. It's on the second floor."

"I don't want to be any trouble," the woman said. "I mean, if the lecture's about to start."

Ronnie just shook her head. "We've got a few minutes." She headed into the break room toward the stairs. Her heels clicked on the flooring, and the electrician, Ethan, looked up from the breaker box beside the refrigerator. "Almost done?" she asked.

"With the alarm, yeah. But…" He trailed off into a shrug, then ran his hands down his legs, as if wiping sweat from his palms.

She frowned. His "but" sounded expensive. "What?"

"You got a short, all right, and I can fix that. But you've got all sorts of problems. Like I told you before, the wiring in this old building is terrible."

Ronnie sighed. As far as she knew, the place had never been rewired. "And that's why the alarm didn't work?"

"I'm surprised anything works." He flashed her a nice

smile. "As my grandpa used to say, you're held together with spit and a prayer."

She laughed. "Story of my life. Okay. I guess I need to just suck it up. Can you fix the short and then give me an estimate on coming in and taking care of everything? No offense, but this piecemeal stuff is really adding up." Over the last year, Ethan had done quite a bit of work throughout the building, but just Band-Aid repairs. She needed to spend the money to do it right once and for all.

She'd already committed to fixing the air conditioner in her apartment. Ethan had taken a look at it that afternoon and deemed it in dire need of parts. She'd authorized the order, of course, but that meant more days of living in a sauna— and then one more large check for the work.

A complete overhaul of the electrical system would be even more expensive, and she certainly didn't need to add to her debt. But she also didn't need the alarm not to trip or a short to spark a fire. Heaven forbid.

After Ethan agreed to get an estimate to her in the next couple of days, she headed to the second floor and pulled the copy of *Tropic of Cancer* from the climate-controlled area. She'd asked Joan to put out all the collectible editions in case anyone who attended the talk wanted to make a purchase, but apparently her assistant hadn't gotten around to it.

With the book in her hand, she headed back to the main room, stepping behind the counter just in time to hear the door jingle. Detective Parker sauntered in, his suit jacket flung carelessly over his shoulder, his tie slightly askew, and his shirt looking remarkably fresh despite the heat. For that matter, the detective looked cool and refreshing, and Ronnie bit the inside of her cheek against the sudden overwhelming urge to take a little dip in *that* pond.

In truth, exploring some of the more enticing parts of the Miller work had been fodder for a secret fantasy that had run through her head all afternoon. She'd selected three passages to discuss in particular, each exploring hidden desires and latent passions. She'd let her imagination run wild, allowing herself the luxury of pretending that Detective Parker figured out she'd selected the text with him in mind…and then insisted on doing a little firsthand investigation of the passages.

Now, though, she realized just how foolish she'd been to start thinking such decadent thoughts. He was yummy, no denying that, but now was not a good time to lose her cool. She was about to stand up in front of a group of eight people and host an informal lecture on Henry Miller. *Henry Miller.* Known for his intimate and explicit descriptions of all things sexual.

What was she thinking inviting this man to watch her lecture? Detective Parker alone was enough to turn her knees to jelly. Combine him with Miller's prose, and she was going to simply melt into the floor and beg him to take her. Not exactly the way to appear scholarly and academic to the small group gathered in her store.

No doubt about it. Ronnie had a serious case of lust.

He crossed the room in two long strides, stopping in front of the counter. She just stood there, silently hoping he couldn't tell the way her nipples had peaked merely upon seeing him again. His brow furrowed as he glanced around, taking in the other people in the room—Marina, Nat, Tommy and a few new faces. "Am I early?"

"Right on time," she said, forcing a businesslike tone. "The lecture's just about to start." She waved a hand toward the meeting area, then handed him a stack of paperbacks. "Give me a hand and pass these out to everyone, okay?"

A flash of surprise crossed Detective Parker's face, but he recovered nicely. "No problem," he said, then headed over and started distributing the books.

She gave him two brownie points for simply going with the flow. She hadn't even realized it herself, but she'd been testing him. So far, he'd passed with flying colors. He'd apologized for the misunderstanding at the police station. He'd admitted to thinking the postcard was a turn-on. He followed directions, willing to let her run this show however she wanted. And—shallow but true—he looked damn good in a starched white shirt.

She stifled a sigh. The bottom line was that she wanted him. Not just as a fantasy, but in the flesh. And she could only hope he wanted more than just her professional assistance.

Because in truth, while a vibrator might be less complicated, Ronnie had a feeling the detective would be a whole lot more fun.

Considering he was technically on duty, Jack's hard-on was really bad form.

He shifted the book, positioning it for better camouflage. The sad part was that after listening dutifully for half an hour, he'd managed to tune out the lecture. No, Jack wasn't getting worked up about the text of Miller's erotic classic. He was getting worked up by the stunning view of Veronica Archer's legs.

She stood in front of the group, the shape of her calves accentuated by the two-inch heels she wore. Barbie-doll shoes, Kelly had called them. His ex had always considered that style of shoe frivolous. If that was the case, Jack was more than willing to raise a toast to frivolity.

The skirt hit just above Veronica's knee, and he could tell she wore no panty hose. He spent a few moments pondering that, his eyes cutting to the top of her thigh, searching for a panty line.

None, and that tailored skirt hugged her like a second skin.

His mouth went a little dry, his cock getting even harder as he pondered the possibilities. A pale pink thong, maybe. Or nothing at all.

Shit. The woman was making him crazy. And hot. It was a good thing he'd stopped by his apartment and ditched the damned vest, or else he'd be burning up.

He shifted in the seat, uncomfortable. He needed to start thinking with his brain again. He was there to learn this stuff, and he forced himself to pay attention.

"—a fictionalized autobiography of his years as an expatriate in Paris," Veronica was saying. "As you probably know, the book was banned for about twenty years in the United States."

She held a copy of the paperback in one hand and the

hardback in the other. "The content of the book is important in the study of erotica," she said, "while the early editions of the book itself are extremely collectible. The book was published with money that Anaïs Nin borrowed, herself well-known for her erotic works."

She put both books down on the table behind her, then pointed to the one in the green-and-white dust jacket and started talking about the number of books that were originally printed. Relatively sure that information wouldn't impact his case, Jack let his mind wander again.

This time, however, he reined in his lust and forced his thoughts to focus on the facts of the case. To wonder about the psychology of a man—he was almost certain the stalker was a man—who would torment women with words meant to be private.

He frowned, questioning his own thought. In fact, the words weren't private at all, they just dealt with sex and he'd colored them with his own values. The words themselves were from books, about as public as you could get. But what, if anything, did that mean to the case?

"We'll talk about Frank Harris next week," Veronica was saying, and Jack made an effort to focus again on her words. "I think you'll find the dichotomy between his work and Miller's interesting. Miller's work lacks pretension and often shocks, whereas Harris had a very romanticized, idealized view of sexuality and women."

She shrugged, the professorial persona falling away as if she'd tossed off a cape. "That's it. Feel free to stay and mingle and ask me any questions you'd like." She addressed the group, but she looked directly at him, then smiled. Jack wondered if there was an unspoken message. At the very least, he intended to stay. He told himself he needed to go over the specific messages with her. And while that was technically accurate, the blaring, inescapable truth was that he simply wanted to get her alone.

One by one the guests greeted her, and he watched their interaction. How many similar lectures took place at bookstores across the city? And did the stalker attend them? Was he in the room right now?

Jack sat up straighter. As was his habit—a byproduct of his profession—he'd already scoped out the room's inhabitants, chatting briefly with them before the lecture started. Now, though, he took a second look, watching the way the audience members interacted with Veronica.

Marina, a stick-thin woman with feathery blond hair, was the first to approach. She seemed fragile and a little lost in her shapeless dress, and Jack wondered if attending Veronica's lectures was the one wild spot in her life. She and Veronica moved together toward the glass case at the front of the store where the cash register sat. As the woman looked at a book Veronica handed her, the college-age kid with freckles and the baggy sweatshirt— Tommy, Jack remembered—wandered in that direction.

Jack hid a smile. *Crush.*

He watched, waiting to see if he'd nailed it. The blonde shook her head and Veronica put the book back behind the counter, looking disappointed. Sure enough, as she slipped out from behind the counter and headed back to mingle, Tommy followed again. But he didn't stop to talk to her himself. Instead, he just watched with big puppy-dog eyes. Definitely a crush.

A few of the other guests approached her with questions, and she chatted with each for as long as they wanted. She did a good job of mingling with her audience, all of whom, Jack realized, were potential customers. She even made a point of saying a few words to Tommy, who looked like he'd died and gone to heaven.

A tall man, probably about Jack's age, was the last to approach, leaving Marina's side to go over and talk to Veronica. He'd come in right as the lecture started, and Jack hadn't met him. Now the man rested his hand on the back of Veronica's shoulder in a gesture of almost possessive familiarity, then bent over and whispered something that made her laugh. Jack's stomach constricted. Then she clasped the guy's hand and lifted up on her toes to kiss him on the cheek.

Against all reason, Jack had the sudden, violent urge to slug the guy.

As lover boy left through the front door, Veronica turned toward Jack. "My brother," she said, nodding toward the door. Relief flowed through him like the slow burn of whiskey.

She leaned casually against the table where he stood. But while her posture was casual, her eyes were intense. "What do you think?" she asked, ostensibly referring to the lecture.

He picked one of the paperbacks off the table, twisting it in his hands. "I thought it was fascinating," he said honestly. "You know your stuff."

Her eyes met his, a silent acknowledgment of his compliment. "But?" she prompted.

He chuckled. The woman was sharp. He wondered if she knew what sort of dangerous territory she was wandering into. Because it wasn't just the case that was on Jack's mind, it was Veronica Archer. And at the moment, he desperately hoped he could combine a little pleasure with his business. "But I'm a little disappointed," he said, taking half a step toward her.

"Oh?" she asked, her voice breathy.

He nodded, moving closer until the subtle scent of her shampoo teased his senses. "The thing is, I was under the impression that I'd be getting *private* lessons."

She smiled, slow and sensual, and he shifted, his slacks suddenly too tight by half.

"Frankly, Detective," she purred, "that's just what I was hoping to hear."

chapter
five

Unfortunately, Ronnie couldn't just tug on the end of Detective Parker's tie, lead him up the stairs to her apartment and have her way with him. Not yet, anyway. She'd stupidly sent Joan home early, and that meant she had to close up the shop.

She flashed an apologetic smile, her eyes darting down to his crotch and back even as she marveled at her own boldness. "Hold that thought, okay? This will only take a few minutes."

His easygoing grin zinged straight to the apex of her thighs, sending a warm flush coursing through her body. She was horny as hell, and all because of this dark-haired detective with eyes so intense she would probably come if he so much as raked his gaze up her body.

With effort, she turned toward the cash register, leaving him to peruse the copy of *Tropic of Cancer* he'd picked up off the table. She licked her lips, wondering which of her flagged passages had engaged his attention.

At the register, she went through her evening checklist, gathering the credit card slips and emptying the register. She put the day's receipts in a bank bag and slid it into the floor safe behind the counter. Normally, she'd make a night deposit. Tonight, she was more interested in the man than the money.

She noticed it as she was standing back up—a single long-stemmed rose on the floor near the window, a note tied to the stem. She plucked it up and read the note— *A rose by any other name.* A grin touched her lips, and she thought of her mysterious admirer. Sweet, but definitely clichéd.

With a little sigh, she put the rose in a drawer, then glanced toward the detective, whimsically wishing he'd confess to leaving the presents. Then again, the little gifts seemed sweet. Innocent. Ronnie didn't want sweet or innocent. Not tonight. Not with Detective Parker.

Joan had left a folder for Ronnie on the counter, and now she flipped through it, making sure there was nothing that needed to be addressed before morning. Nothing. Just a few more notes for the catalog and Joan's weekly I-shoulda-been-in-PR memo. With a low chuckle, Ronnie rolled her eyes.

Detective Parker cocked his head, a question in his gaze. She lifted the paper in silent response, then slipped it back into the folder.

"Joke-of-the-month club?" he asked.

"Pretty much," Ronnie said. "A note from my assistant

on how to increase traffic to the store. I think she's a little worried about job security." The moment she said the words, she regretted them. She wanted to sleep with this man, not discuss the store's precarious financial position.

"Having some tight times?" he said.

She shrugged. "Who isn't? We'll survive. We've been in the red before. The vagaries of running a business."

He nodded, heading toward her with the book still in his hand. He moved with athletic power and grace, and when he reached her side, she'd already forgotten her momentary lapse into monetary worries. "Can I help?" he asked.

She blinked. "The business?"

He laughed, the sound warm and genuine. "I don't think I'd be much help there. I meant now. Closing up."

She shook her head. "No. I'm almost done."

"Good." He smiled and her heart picked up its tempo. "Because I'm getting anxious to start my lesson."

She swallowed, delighted by the suggestive tone of his words. "I thought we would work upstairs. Maybe have a bite."

A grin eased across his face, slow and confident. "A bite sounds great."

She swallowed, certain he was talking about more than just food. She took a deep breath, telling herself this was what she wanted, and hoping like hell she wasn't misinterpreting signals. "The air conditioner doesn't work, so it's hot as hell, but we can open the windows over the fire escape and get a breeze."

"I can handle the heat," he assured her.

She met his smile, and her pulse picked up tempo as she led the way to the stairs. Raw desire mixed with nerves. A dangerous combination.

He held the door open for her, his arm extending up the solid wood in a gesture that practically oozed sensuality and sin. She took an unsteady breath, hoping she wasn't making a mistake inviting him to her apartment.

If the evening went the way she wanted, *that* wouldn't be a mistake. But if they really did just eat and talk… well, she wasn't certain she'd be able to survive the disappointment.

Ronnie had always thought her kitchen was perfect. Nice and cozy, with just the right amount of cabinet and counter space.

She'd been wrong.

Now, standing in the room with Detective Parker only a few feet away, she realized just how small the space was. He filled it up. All six feet something of him. But it wasn't just size. He had a presence that took over. As if he belonged there and always had.

A little bit disconcerting, it was also a turn-on. The air was charged with his masculine aura, and the heat he was generating sizzled in her veins.

"*Lady Chatterley, The Boudoir,* and some miscellaneous postcards, artist unknown." He'd spread a photocopy of each piece of evidence across the counter, and now he held his hands out in surrender. "I'm at a loss. Do you see a connection?"

"Not really," she said. She sliced into a juicy apple, arranging the pieces on a plate with Brie and crackers. "I mean, other than that it's all erotica. And not to sound arrogant, but I'm pretty familiar with that particular stuff, so I think that if there was a connection, I'd get it."

"What makes you so sure?"

She shrugged, then wiped her hands on a towel before tugging open the refrigerator door. "You saw the postcards," she said. "We have quite a collection—both collectible and not." She pulled out a bowl of red seedless grapes. "How about these?" she asked.

He nodded, and she slid the bowl onto the counter. The heat was stifling, even with the slight cross breeze, and so they'd decided against actually cooking.

"Plus, I did my master's thesis on D. H. Lawrence," she continued. "And *The Boudoir* has always been a favorite of mine." She shoved an expired carton of milk aside and reached for a chilled bottle of unopened German wine. "Piesporter?" she asked.

He took the bottle. "Corkscrew?"

She pointed to a drawer, and he went to work on the cork. "I've done a couple of lectures on both," she said. She lifted her hair up off her neck, then let it fall back down, the tiny waft of air slightly refreshing on her damp skin. "Too bad you didn't know me a few weeks ago," she said. "Then you'd already know this stuff."

The cork slid neatly from the bottle. "Too bad indeed," he said, but she got the feeling he wasn't talking about the lectures and allowed herself a tiny smile.

She cut a few more slices of apple and arranged them neatly on the plate. Apple slices, oranges, grapes and

Brie. She wished she'd gone to the market recently. Even more, she wished her kitchen were stocked with mangoes. Pomegranates. Nice juicy peaches.

She licked her lips, her thoughts drifting from delectable fruits to one delicious detective. Oh, yeah, she had it bad. But business before pleasure and all that jazz. She only hoped the pleasure part of the equation was on Detective Parker's agenda.

Determined to present at least the appearance of professionalism, she carried the plate from the kitchen into her living room. The room was spare, just a coffee table and a couch. Not even a television, since she kept her small black-and-white in the bedroom, turned at a slight angle so that she could watch it from either the desk or the bed.

The unintended benefit of the sparse furnishings was that he would have no choice but to sit next to her on the couch. If he sat at all. The detective seemed more interested in the framed prints on her wall.

"These are quite…interesting," he said. He inched closer, as if drawn in by the passionate images of the prints.

"They're Japanese," she said. They were high-quality lithographs she'd bought at a gallery on the Upper East Side many years ago. She'd blown a year's worth of savings, but even at that, the prints were nowhere near as expensive as what an original would have cost. "Many experts consider *shunga* prints to be some of the most extraordinary works of erotic art ever created."

Parker's jaw tightened as his gaze skimmed from one print to the other, landing on the largest of the set—a woman and man, dressed in traditional garb. The woman hugged the trunk of a tree, her face alight with passion as the man, completely dressed except for his bare feet and his penis, brushed aside her clothing and entered her from behind.

She pointed toward the image. "This one is from the mid-1600s. The original, I mean. It's particularly interesting when you compare the overall feel of the picture with the general philosophy of the culture."

He shifted, turning to look at her just enough so that she could tell he was interested, and not merely being polite while she warmed to her topic.

"A seventeenth-century French writer once saw some *shunga* prints, and commented that they showed the animal frenzies of the flesh. Furious copulation and rage."

Parker nodded, still examining the prints' vibrant images. "I can see that."

"Right," she said, moving to stand behind him and looking at the images over his shoulder. "But Japanese erotic texts show how much respect for the sexual act is inherent in the culture. *The Pillow Book*—that's sort of like Japan's twelfth-century *The Joy of Sex*—taught that the gods smile upon lovemaking, and that if the man and the woman are both satisfied, then the gods are satisfied."

He shifted, turning to face her directly. "Is that right?" His low voice eased down her spine.

She swallowed, her composure fading under his steady gaze. "Um, yes. In a lot of ways, the roots of erotica stem back to the intersection of sex and spirituality." She rolled one shoulder. "Sex was considered a gift from God, and it was like a sin not to know how to pleasure your mate."

She'd automatically slid into her professorial tone, and she cringed. "I don't mean to lecture...."

He shook his head, just slightly. "No, I like it. The information and the philosophy. I definitely came to the right place." Again, that fabulous smile. "And for all the right reasons."

She licked her lips, suddenly self-conscious. "This *is* my profession," she said. "And it's always been an interest of mine. But it's not my only interest." She didn't know why it was important that he understand that. He wanted her professional help, and she wanted...well, she wanted *him*. And, yes, that meant sex. But for some reason she wanted him to realize that there was more to her.

She sat on the edge of her sofa and picked up a grape. "I mean, I have Disney animation cells framed in my bathroom," she said. "And if I had to choose between *9 1/2 Weeks* and *Die Hard*, Bruce Willis would win out every time."

"I'm a *Matrix* fan myself," he said. He moved away from the wall and came to perch on the edge of her coffee table, right in front of her. "Although, there is that ice-cube scene in *9 1/2 Weeks*...."

She shivered. There certainly was. And her apartment was so damn hot.

She shook her head, banishing the thought, then cleared her throat. "So what is it you need help with?"

"Honestly? That's part of the problem. I'm not entirely sure."

Her brow furrowed, her eyes going to the file folder of evidence he'd tossed on the table.

He followed her gaze. "That, of course. But more than that I need..." He trailed off, standing up and tugging at his tie, as if he could think better without the silk noose around his neck. He pulled it loose, and it slipped out from his collar. He draped it over the back of her couch, and for some reason, Ronnie couldn't take her eyes off of it. That one tiny piece of silk seemed to loom large in the room.

What else might he take off to beat the heat?

As if in answer to her question, he unbuttoned the top two buttons on his shirt. A smattering of chest hair peeked through, and she clenched her fist against the urge to reach out, finish the job on his buttons and run her fingers over his firm, hard chest.

Focus, Ronnie. She popped the grape into her mouth, chewed and swallowed. "What, Detective? What do you need?" She tilted her head to the side. "Or more specifically, why do you need me?"

"Now, there's a loaded question." His slow smile teased her, the gesture full of decadent possibilities. "Why do I need you...?" He trailed off, then sat again on the table, this time taking a slice of orange. He bit into it, the liquid clinging to his mouth.

Ronnie licked her own lips, letting his question linger in the air between them.

"I need specific information, yes. But other than showing you the pieces of evidence and having you spill out everything you know, I'm at a loss for what else I should be doing."

"I can do that," she said. "Just start rattling on about *Lady Chatterley's Lover, The Boudoir,* and the postcards."

"I know," he said. His tone was professional, but his eyes told a different story. His eyes held desire—and Ronnie held his gaze. "It may come to that."

"In the meantime, how can I help?"

He leaned forward. "I need to know this stuff. Really know it." His eyes met hers. "Know it like you do."

"Immersion," she said.

"What?"

She smiled. "You need to immerse yourself in the same way they teach languages now."

"Immersion," he repeated, his voice barely a murmur. "I like the sound of that." He pressed his hand on her leg, his palm cupping her bare knee, the tips of his fingers just under the hem of her skirt. "And you'll be my teacher?"

"I said I would."

"Total immersion?"

"Yes." One word, but it offered so much.

With his eyes locked on hers, he reached behind him, his fingers finding the paperback he'd tossed carelessly there earlier.

She exhaled, disappointed. She'd hoped for a different kind of immersion. At least right now. The temperature, the proximity, the subject matter, each teased and taunted her. The sullen heat of the apartment pressed around her, making her antsy. She didn't want to lecture, didn't want to think. She was wired and frantic for release.

He cracked the spine on the paperback, then flipped the pages, clearly looking for a passage.

Apparently she and the detective weren't quite on the same wavelength.

"I was reading this earlier," he said. "It seems like as good a place to start with my immersion lessons as any."

Something in his voice gave her pause, and she simply nodded, silently urging him to continue.

"I was thinking about the language," he said. As he spoke, his finger stroked the soft skin above her knee. "It's powerful. Intense." His whole body leaned forward, and his hand moved along with it, sliding up under her skirt along her inner thigh.

She gasped, the unexpected thrust of his fingertips against her soft flesh both startling and welcome.

"Provocative," he continued. "I'm thinking perhaps I should immerse myself in this."

"I, um, I know what passage you're reading." *Her* passage. The one she'd fantasized about. The passage she'd imagined exploring with him.

She licked her lips, remembering Miller's explicit language. Could her fantasy really be coming true? Did the detective really intend to act it out?

"And yet there's a vulgar quality to the language, too," the detective said.

"Yes...yes, there is," she said. "Miller's famous for his raw words."

Parker slid to the ground, dropping to his knees in front of her. She sucked in a breath in anticipation. *This was happening. Really and truly happening.*

"Just like you said. Almost like an instruction manual." He placed his hands on her, one on each knee, and urged her legs apart.

She tensed, surprised by the bold movement, even though a tiny part of her had seen it coming—had wished for it, even. The linen of her tailored skirt pressed into the flesh of her thigh, restricting her movement. She shifted on the couch, trying to inch the skirt higher and allow him to push her legs farther apart.

Though she tried to be subtle, the movement was wanton, almost desperate. Already, she was wet, and her sex throbbed, as if all she needed was his touch to complete an intricate puzzle. Her nipples were tight under the thin lace bra, and she arched her back in an almost unconscious invitation, silently begging him to flick his tongue over her breast.

Slowly, too slowly, he ran his hands along her thighs, his thumbs still tracing the soft inside flesh. As his hands drew upward, he took her skirt, as well. She held her breath, her head back, her eyes closed.

The air in the apartment was hot, but it felt cool against the dense, damp curls at the apex of her thighs. In testament to her fantasy, she hadn't worn underwear, but she'd never truly expected that he'd find out. Now he did, and she knew the exact moment he realized. She heard a low, almost strangled intake of breath. Then felt a thin, directed stream of cool air as he blew gently on her clit.

She almost came right then.

"Oh, yes," she whispered. Her hips rose, seeking more. Seeking release.

"I was right," he whispered, his voice raw. "No under-wear."

"Good or bad?" she asked, barely able to form words.

"Very, very good."

Sighing, she reached for him, but he pressed her hand back into the base of the couch. "Later," he said. "Right now, we're studying."

She smiled slightly. At this school, she was willing to be a permanent student.

"It's not entirely like Miller," he said. "She was on a chair, not a sofa."

Ronnie swallowed. She knew the passage…she knew what was coming.

"And she wasn't wearing a stitch of clothes," Parker continued. His hands roamed her thighs, higher and higher, but never quite touching where she wanted to be touched.

He managed to ease the skirt all the way up, though, and she was bare from her hips down, the skirt bunched around her waist. Naked and hot and needy

His thumbs grazed her pubic hair, the slight motion sending tremors through her body. She drew her hands up, cupping her own breasts, imagining his hands on her and his cock deep inside.

"What did he do then?" Parker asked.

She licked her lips, not entirely sure she could speak. "Is this a pop quiz?"

"Absolutely." With the pad of his thumb, he traced down over her slick heat. But it was just a tease, and she moaned in protest. "What?" he repeated. "What did he do?"

"Spread her open," she said, the words both an answer and a demand.

"Like this?" He explored her with the tips of his fingers, just like in the book. Her body thrummed, her nerves near to shattering, and she pressed down against his hand in a rhythmic motion that was utterly out of her control.

"And then what?" Parker asked.

But she couldn't answer. Her mouth was too dry, her body too alive, and her sex too damn wet. She couldn't think, didn't want to think. She only wanted him. Right then. All of him.

Apparently, he knew, and he took pity on her. "This?" he asked. But before she had a chance to answer, he dipped down, burying his face between her legs, spreading them wide. With his tongue he stroked her clit, his finger deep inside her warm, wet folds.

The pleasure built and built like rising waves, and she wanted to ride that surf forever. But she was too worked up already, and with one more thrust of his tongue, the storm hit, her body clenching him tight as the orgasm shot through her on wave after wave of unbearable pleasure.

Her body sagged, still tingly and sensitive, but no longer on the brink of nuclear meltdown. He pulled back to look at her, his eyes dark like liquid sin.

"Well?" he asked. "How's my interpretation of Henry Miller?"

"You get an A," she whispered.

He grinned, and her heartbeat tripped.

He rose then, urging her up with him. His arm slipped

around her waist, and he held her close, then pressed his lips over hers. At first soft and gentle, he soon coaxed her lips apart. The kiss heated, like a brushfire slow to ignite, but wild and deep and dangerous once it got going.

When he broke the kiss, he brushed a finger over her cheek, the simple gesture suggesting that this was only an appetizer.

Fine by her.

Ronnie drew in a breath, long and steadying. Her lips tingled from the force of his kiss, and she clung to him. Her body moved ever so slightly, undulating against him, the motion instinctual. Primitive. *Raw.*

He cupped her rear with his palms, pressing her closer, his erection stiff against her thigh. "Veronica," he whispered, his voice raw and needy.

"Call me Ronnie," she said. She eased closer, her body rubbing against his as she lifted onto her toes. She knew him only as Detective Parker, and suddenly that wasn't enough. She swallowed, unsure.

They both wanted the sex, there was certainly no question about that. But they'd never spoken of it. Not really. They'd just done it. Some of it, anyway. Now she wanted more, or at least the possibility of more. And she wanted it badly enough that she was willing to risk breaking their unspoken rules.

Gently, she brushed her lips over his, then leaned back. "Shall I just call you Detective?" she asked, trying to keep her voice light.

Those penetrating gray eyes looked deep into her soul. "Is that what you want?"

She licked her lips. "I want to know your name."

Something flashed in his eyes. "Jack," he said.

She exhaled, then smiled. "Make love to me, Jack. Make love to me right now."

Make love to me, Jack.

Oh, yeah. That's exactly what he intended to do.

With a low groan, he clutched her bare ass, his fingertips pressed into the soft flesh as he urged her closer. His cock throbbed with the need to sink into her, deep and fast and furious. And as she writhed against him, her little breathless noises teasing and tugging at his senses, he wondered if he could even last that long.

Make love to me, Jack.

He swallowed, dipping his head down as he ran his tongue over the delicate curve of her ear, her words echoing in his head. Familiar words. From other women, other lovers. But never with quite the same impact.

There was something about Veronica Archer—her touch, her scent, her everything—all combining to drive him to the brink of madness. What had she called it? Animal frenzy? That was how she made him feel. Frenzied and hot and hard and desperate.

Her breasts pressed against his chest, her tight, hard nipples firm against him. He reached up, his fingers fumbling uselessly at the tiny buttons on the front of her shirt.

"Rip it off," she whispered, her voice unsteady.

He didn't argue, just gave the delicate material a tug. A sharp tearing sound, and then his hand against warm flesh and cool lace. Her bra was flimsy, and he pushed the material down, freeing her plump breast. With his thumb and forefinger, he stroked the deep, brown areola, watching with delight as the tender flesh puckered even more, her nipple tightening perceptively.

"Do you like that?" he whispered.

"Yes." She clutched his shoulders, her answering murmur holding no hesitation.

"What about this?" he asked, even as he slid his hand down her ass, his fingers seeking her heat. She was wet, a warm, slick heat, and he felt her body tighten, closing around his finger as he searched for her core.

She arched her back, her butt tilting up, giving him easier access, and he groaned, low in his throat. The sound of a starving man who'd just stumbled on a buffet of ambrosia.

"Jack." Her voice was hoarse, little more than a whisper, as she bucked against his hand, urging him inside her. Harder, deeper. Her hands fumbled at his fly, her scrambling fingers on the thin material driving him to the brink.

Lord, he was going to explode.

With one swift move, he spun her in his arms, then urged her to her knees, facing the sofa. He pushed the table backward with the heel of his foot, and it slid out of the way, giving him room to kneel behind her. He finished her work on his slacks, hurrying out of them and his boxers. At the last minute, he remembered protection, and he scrambled for his wallet, hoping like hell there was a stray condom still in the window behind his driver's license.

Success, and he slipped it on, then knelt behind her. She knew what he had in mind, and bent forward at the waist, her chest and stomach pressed flat against the sofa cushion, the rest of her right there for him.

He teased her first, clutching her hips as he stroked her wet folds with the tip of his cock. But that teased him, too, and he was too hard, too ready. With one quick thrust, he entered her.

The cool flesh of her rear pressed against him, and with each thrust, he sank deeper into heaven. She tightened around him, milking him, her body's reaction just as enticing as her low moans of pleasure. He clung to her, his hands cupping her breasts, as over and over he thrust.

She moved against him, his skin sliding over hers, dewy with sweat from the thick heat of the apartment. She smelled like soap and sex, the combination intoxicating.

She whispered his name, the breathy sound of her voice urging him on. Not that he needed urging. He couldn't have stopped if his life depended on it. And he thrust deeper and harder, the pressure building and building until he couldn't fight it anymore.

He groaned, and his entire body shook with the force of his orgasm. He sagged against her in satisfied exhaustion, holding her close as they curled over the side of the couch. He kissed the back of her neck, her ear, her cheek.

"Mmm," she said. "That was amazing."

"Yes, it was," he said, nipping at her ear. He knew he should feel some twinge of guilt, some hint of something. After all, he was a cop and she was a consultant. But he didn't feel anything but happy and satisfied. And what the hell? He'd been putting in twenty-hour days for weeks. The case was pressing down around him, and his body craved the release.

And besides, he deserved a break. Hell, he deserved a bonus.

Ronnie shifted in his arms, and he smiled. *His* bonus. He sure as hell couldn't complain. They were consenting adults. And, frankly, he hoped she'd consent again. And again. And again.

He stroked his fingers idly up and down her back, tracing over the thin silk of her now-ruined blouse.

"Just think," she said, her voice muffled against the pillow. "That was with our clothes half on. Do you think we'd survive if we got naked?"

His groin tightened, and he said a silent thank-you. "I'm willing to try it if you are."

She turned her head, her eyes meeting his, her expression playful yet serious. "Oh yeah," she said. "I'm willing."

chapter
six

"You got laid." Donovan slid into the chair across from Jack's desk. "Son of a bitch."

Jack scowled but didn't deny it. He might not have chosen so coarse a euphemism, but the end result was the same. "Any luck on the typewriter?"

Donovan barked out a laugh, obviously amused at the change of subject, then nodded. "Possibly. Our guy's ninety-nine percent sure it was typed on a Royal. An old model, like from around World War II."

"Well, that's something." Jack rubbed his temples. "What about fibers? Forensics find anything interesting in the Crawley apartment?"

Donovan shook his head. "Nothing we've heard about yet." He took a sip of coffee. "So what have you got on for today? I need to go interview a bouncer in the Andretti case."

Jack nodded. Melissa Andretti had been brutally raped.

Unfortunately for Miss Andretti, she worked as a stripper in one of the sleazier joints around town. Which meant nothing in the eyes of the law, but often could color a juror's perception. It was Jack and Donovan's job to hand the tightest case possible to the district attorney's office so they could prosecute the rapist and avoid putting the victim on trial.

"Unless you're gunning for company, I'm going to stay here," Jack said. "I'm still on call in the Bleeker matter, and I've got a list of calls to make for Andretti. Plus, Veronica Archer gave me homework." He handed Donovan the illustrated anthology of erotica Ronnie had pressed into his hand as he'd left that morning.

"Well, well," his partner said, passing the book back. "I see you've got a rough day ahead."

Jack just rolled his eyes and picked up the phone, dialing the first number on his notes for Melissa Andretti's case.

Chuckling, Donovan grabbed his stuff and headed out.

By lunch, Jack had learned little relating to the Andretti rape and decided it was time to move on to erotica. With a bowl of microwaved ravioli in front of him, he opened the anthology and started skimming the pages.

Not a good idea.

Every page reminded him of Veronica. His senses were on overdrive, her scent teasing him, the feel of her skin lingering on his fingertips. Last night had to have been the most overwhelming sexual experience of his life, in no small part because of the "educational" component.

Trying to study now was an exercise in futility. At least his desk hid the evidence of the way his mind was wandering.

He closed the book and shifted in his chair, then drummed his fingers on the desk and stared at the phone. After a moment's hesitation, he reached for the handset and dialed.

She answered on the first ring. "Archer's Rare Books and Manuscripts. How may I help you?"

"Ronnie?"

"Well, hey there," she said, her voice losing the businesslike tone. "How's your day?"

He felt a smile cross his face and felt a little silly. But he liked her asking. It felt...nice. "It started out great," he said, remembering the way she'd pressed against him in bed. "It's been going downhill ever since."

"Maybe it'll pick up again this evening," she said, her voice just a little too innocent.

"I can always hope," he said.

She laughed. "Have you been studying? There might be a pop quiz tonight."

"I do great on quizzes," he said.

"Yeah. I bet you do."

"What time?" he asked, looking at the clock and willing the hands to turn faster.

"Later, I'm afraid. I need to run some errands after I close up. How about nine-thirty? I should be back by then."

"Oh." Disappointment clung to him like some living thing. "No problem."

"Unless you'd like to come with me?" The words were

casual, but he thought he heard a hint of eagerness in her voice, as if she hoped he'd take her up on the invitation.

Then again, that might just be wishful thinking. The possibility depressed him, and he wondered at his own disappointment. He realized how much the idea bothered him that he might be reading more into her words and tone than was really there, and that she didn't really want to spend time with him outside of the bedroom.

He ran his fingers through his hair, frustrated with himself. He'd started out needing nothing more than help from this woman. He'd moved quickly into wanting her help with a healthy dose of sex. And now...? Now he wasn't sure anymore. All he knew was that Ronnie pushed his buttons. But, hey, they were good together, and he wanted to see where this thing between them might lead.

"I can't imagine you would want to come," she said, filling the silence he'd left hanging between them. "It'll probably bore you to tears. I've got to get a wedding present for my best friend from college. And I want to get something for her little girl, as well. Second marriage," she added before he could ask. "I figure Delaney will be feeling weird and should get a present, too."

On a normal day, Jack would rather scrub his toilet than shop for toys and wedding paraphernalia. This was not a normal day. "Sure," he said. "Sounds great."

"Really? Wonderful." She didn't give him a chance to change his mind. "Meet me here at eight." He heard a customer approach, and she said a quick goodbye, then hung up.

He replaced the handset and stared at the phone. *Shopping*. What the hell was he thinking?

Ronnie was in a crappy mood, and even the prospect of seeing Jack again didn't help. She perched on a stool behind the counter, her laptop open, scrolling through the spreadsheets that showed the store's financial condition.

Today there'd been a nice little influx of cash—Marina had returned for the Miller edition. But even with that shot in the arm, the store's balance sheet was bleeding red. The problem was simple cash flow—more was flowing out than in.

Not a good economic plan for a retail business, and the fact that she didn't have any brilliant solution only made her mood darker. Even Nat's entrance didn't lighten her mood. She looked up from the computer and gave him a halfhearted wave.

"Good to see you, too," he said, sounding a little surly.

She squinted at him. "What's wrong?"

"Not a damn thing," he said. "What's wrong on your end? I mean, I thought you'd be grinning from ear to ear and humming some jaunty tune." His tone was light, almost too light.

"Not hardly." She frowned. "And why would you think that, anyway?"

"I live one floor above you, McDonald." A muscle in his cheek twitched. "Thin walls."

A spark of anger fired in her belly. She loved her brother, but he'd never once approved of her boyfriends.

"The last time I checked, I was over twenty-one," she said, her bad mood gathering steam.

Nat just glowered.

"Oh, for crying out loud, Nat. You can quit playing daddy, okay? I can take care of myself."

"I only wanted you to make sure this place was safe, Ron." His voice dripped with sarcasm. "All that required was *talking* with the police…"

"It's really none of your business." She lifted her chin. "Besides, he came to me. He's got a case and he needs help. Finding out about the robbery is just a perk." Plus, a hefty dose of Detective Jack Parker had been just what the doctor ordered. And even better, she genuinely liked him. So what was there to be embarrassed about? Hell, the one bright spot in the day had been when he'd called.

Nat headed into the break room, grabbed a soda from the fridge, then returned. He popped the top, took a long sip and looked at her dubiously. "The cops are asking for your help? With what?"

"With erotica. There's a stalker in town."

His blank expression quickly turned to one of surprise, then moved on to concern. "Are you okay? Does it involve you?"

She shook her head. "No, of course not. I'm just helping him understand the genre." She looked defiantly at her brother. "And I happen to like the man, so let's leave it at that."

He didn't answer, just took another long pull on his soda, then tapped his finger against the side of the can.

"Oh, come on," she said, irritated. "You should be

happy. My own personal detective, so now I have the inside scoop and know that they don't have a single lead on the robbery. No news, and no reason to think our thief will be back. So now you can catch your plane. Have a good time and take lots of pictures." She looked at her watch, a ridiculous habit since his plane didn't leave until the morning. "Are you packed?"

He shot her another odd glance, which she assumed stemmed from the fact that she was switching from being mothered to mothering him. "Pretty much," he finally said. "The plane leaves at the crack of dawn, so I doubt I'll see you in the morning."

"You'll call?"

He nodded. "You'll be careful?"

She wasn't sure if he was worried about the stalker or the detective, but either way the answer was the same. "Of course."

He sighed, then shook his head. "You really should just sell the place," he said, obviously needing to have the last word. "It's a damn money pit."

Ronnie clenched her fists, not willing to go there again. "Have a great trip," she said mildly.

"Thanks," he responded, but his look said he knew she was avoiding the topic. Thankfully, the front door buzzer rang, and she was saved from having to get into yet another endless conversation about why they should sell the building and split the money.

Old-fashioned blinds hung over the closed door, and she pushed them aside, delighted to see Jack on the other side of the glass. She twisted the dead bolt and pulled the door open. He strode in, his hand immediately reaching up to loosen his tie.

"I think it's as hot in here as it is out there," he said.

"It is pretty damn hot," Nat said.

Ronnie shot him a look that she hoped conveyed maximum irritation. "Jack, this is my brother, Nat." She gestured between the two men, who shook hands, eyeing each other like two alpha wolves. "Nat, Jack is the detective I was telling you about. Detective Parker."

"So nice to see you're on the case," Nat said. "Protecting my sister and all that."

His tone was perfectly polite, but Ronnie wasn't fooled. Her perpetually charming brother was being a jerk. He didn't usually display this character trait, but she wasn't about to jump in and psychoanalyze him right then. "Nat's on his way out," she said.

"Dinner plans," Nat said. "But I'll be here in the morning. I've got a plane to catch." He looked Jack up and down. "Maybe I'll see you on the stairs around 5:00 a.m."

Jack didn't miss a beat. "Maybe you will," he said. He took a step to stand beside Ronnie and wove his fingers into hers. She ducked her head toward the ground, sure her cheeks had bloomed all shades of pink. Great. Nat was being a jerk, and she'd turned into a blushing sixteen-year-old. No one was who they seemed anymore.

Nat scowled but offered no retort.

"Come on," Ronnie said. She took a deep breath to gather herself, then let go of Jack's hand and hustled Nat toward the door. "I'm going to lock up behind you." As soon as her brother was safely on the street, she turned back to Jack. She aimed what she hoped was an endearing smile in his direction. "Sorry about that. We tried to housebreak him, but failed."

Jack's smile broadened, revealing a hint of dimple under the five o'clock shadow. "He's just watching out for his sister."

She frowned, adjusting her glasses. "I guess. He's usually not like this."

"Like what?"

Ronnie waved the question away. "It doesn't matter. He just got a fabulous gig, and he's probably nervous." She smiled up at him. "I don't intend to let my brother ruin what I fully intend to be a wonderful evening."

Shopping off a registry was usually a tedious bore, but Ronnie was having a wonderful time. It wasn't that Karen's registry was that entertaining, though. It was the company.

Jack.

Unlike some men, he didn't hang out near the door, looking mildly ill and taking frequent peeks at his wrist-watch. No, after an initial warning that he wasn't the best company on a shopping trip, he'd gone and proceeded to prove himself a liar.

"This," he said, pointing to a food processor that looked like it had been invented by former NASA scientists. "See, *this* is something you need in a real kitchen. Not that pansy-ass processor on your list."

Ronnie glanced at the Williams-Sonoma salesperson, wondering if she'd taken offense at the "pansy-ass" comment. But she was just standing back, smiling benignly. Considering Jack's selected model cost at least two hundred more than the item on the registry, Jack was probably on her favorite-person list.

"But that's not the one they registered for," Ronnie pointed out.

"*She* registered for. Trust me, babe. A guy did not purposefully pass up this model. Look." He pointed to all the accessories. "Detachable blades. More power. A bigger reservoir. If the guy's going to cook, this is what he wants in his kitchen."

She laughed, feeling as if she'd walked into a cross between *Tool Time* and *Martha Stewart*. "Maybe I should just get them a lasagna dish," she said.

He shrugged. "Wimp."

She aimed a coy smile in his direction. "I'm just not certain I can handle all that power."

He took her hand, his fingers sliding between hers. "Believe me. You can."

Her cheeks warmed, and the salesgirl walked a respectable distance ahead of them, giving the illusion, at least, that she didn't know what was going on. Just to change the subject, Ronnie picked up a pepper mill, about two feet long, made from teak or mahogany or some equally expensive wood. "What do you think?"

The corner of his mouth curved up, and his eyes sparkled devilishly. He moved in closer, his mouth almost brushing her ear. "Phallic," he said. "I think you're thinking what I'm thinking."

She gasped, her body warming both from the invitation in his words and a little burst of embarrassment. Her first reaction was to toss the mill on the table and run to flatware. Forks seemed safe. Forks. Forking. Nope. Not safe at all.

Damn.

She drew in a breath and willed herself to play it cool. Slowly and deliberately, she stroked the mill, her eyes meeting his. "High quality," she said. "Hard wood. Very hard." She trailed her fingers over it, up and down, watching as his eyes changed, shifting from his victory to his ultimate defeat.

She laughed, delighted. "Don't bet against a woman who studies erotica, Jack," she said. "You can't win."

"True," he conceded. "But at least when I lose, I win."

Finally, they settled on a pasta press, then took a taxi to FAO Schwarz. Ronnie figured that store, at least, was safe territory. No chance that they'd end up in an erotic battle of words over teddy bears.

As it turned out, Ronnie was half right and half wrong. Jack made no sultry suggestions, passed off no intimate touches. Instead, he walked with her through the store, his hand holding hers, as they argued mildly over the best present for a five-year-old.

After much haggling, he finally convinced her to get a princess dress-up kit, complete with tiara and scepter. "Lots of cousins," he said to explain his authority in this area. "This store gets my Christmas paycheck."

"Do you have a lot of brothers and sisters?" Ronnie asked.

Jack shook his head. "Nope. Just me. But my mom

has five brothers and my dad has three sisters. And all of their kids have kids." He smiled. "I'm the black sheep. Over thirty years old. Unmarried. No kids. It's a travesty."

She laughed. "Well, you sound hopeless to me."

"Stay away from my family," he said, pointing a mock stern finger at her. "Talk like that will only bolster their fear that I'm never going to settle down."

"Will you?" she asked as they continued to stroll through the rows of toys. "Settle down, I mean?" The second she said the words, she regretted them. Not exactly appropriate conversation when they'd just started dating. Especially when she wasn't certain that what they were doing *was* dating.

"Absolutely," he said, without missing a beat. "I've been burned a few times, I'll admit that. But eventually I want what my parents have. Fifty years next month."

"Wow," she said. She squinted at him. "And you said you're over thirty, right?"

He laughed. "Don't say it," he said. "You'll sound like my mom. If I want a golden anniversary, I'd better get busy." He shrugged. "Honestly, it's not the years. It's the way they are together. Comfortable, like best friends, but they still hold hands. You can see it in their eyes—they're crazy about each other."

"That's so great," she said.

"I take it from your tone that your parents weren't exactly love bugs?"

"My mom split when I was little. I barely remember her. My dad was pretty cool, but he was more interested in running the store. Nat's always been the constant in my life." She pulled a teddy bear from a display and hugged it to her chest.

"No other family?"

She shook her head. "I was married once," she said. "It didn't take."

He looked as if he was going to ask her about Burt, but then he just nodded, continuing through the aisles.

"Is your family nearby?" she asked, steering the discussion back.

"I've got a few cousins in Jersey," he said. A flicker of something indefinable crossed his face. Anger? Sadness? Ronnie didn't know, but the expression was gone in an instant.

"Jack?"

He squeezed her hand. "I grew up in Jersey. But my parents are in Palm Beach now. And I've got relatives all up and down the coast. Driving Highway 95 is pretty much like going on a mobile Parker family reunion."

He took the teddy bear from her and gave it an appraising glance. "Are you buying this little guy?"

"No, I think I'll stick with the dress-up set."

"I think I will, then. He looks like he could use a good home, and Melinda starts kindergarten next month. She could probably use a new friend."

"Yeah," Ronnie said. "I bet she could."

He took her hand as they continued to browse, now looking for something for Melinda's brother, so he wouldn't feel left out.

Ronnie hid a smile. A man earnestly buying toys for

his little cousins might not be seductive, but it was very, very sexy. And sweet.

Had she really once told herself she wanted hot sex and nothing more? She was either a liar or taking full advantage of a woman's prerogative to change her mind. Because she wanted more. Despite the inevitable complications and the possibility of severe heartache, she really did. And she wanted it with Jack Parker.

She pressed a light kiss to his cheek.

He looked at her, a question in his eyes. But she just shrugged and took the costume to the checkout stand. Later, she'd tell him just how sexy he was.

For that matter, she'd show him.

Until he'd met Veronica Archer, Jack had never considered taxis particularly sexy.

He'd been an idiot.

Now he was clued in to the truth—taxis were a gift box of sensual possibilities wrapped up in steel and four wheels.

They'd hailed a cab outside of the toy store and climbed into the back. It was a big car, a luxury vehicle that had suffered too many potholes and turned too many sharp corners. A gray plastic divider separated them from the driver, providing at least the illusion of privacy.

The illusion was all they needed.

As soon as they pulled into traffic, Ronnie had scooted to his side, her hand pressed lightly on his thigh. Moving slower than molasses, she'd inched her hand up, her movements shielded by the shopping bag resting on his lap.

He'd shot her a look of mock warning, but she'd just responded with wide, innocent eyes. But while her eyes might be innocent, her hand was anything but. Slowly, with deliberate purpose, she pressed her hand over his cock, rubbing in slow, intimate circles.

Now he was hard as a rock, his body ready to spring on her like a tiger from a trap.

But while he was a tiger, Ronnie was as cool as the Cheshire cat.

"Dangerous," he whispered, forcing the word out.

Her smile twitched. "I hope so," she said, her fingers maneuvering his zipper down.

He cast a glance toward the driver, who looked to be concentrating on the traffic. Jack wondered if that wasn't a ruse. Then Ronnie's hand slipped inside his pants, her warm fingers circling his cock, and Jack decided he really didn't give a damn what the driver was doing.

She stroked him, the slow, rhythmic movements driving him crazy but not taking him to the edge. His body trembled, but she knew just how far to go, just how much he could stand. Precisely how to drive him crazy.

She wore a wraparound skirt, and he slipped his hand through the slit in the material, his hand closing over her damp panties. She whimpered, a low noise in her throat, and he had to force himself not to come right then.

She met his eyes, holding his gaze as her tongue swept over her lips, leaving them glistening. She raised an eyebrow. "Guess where I want you to kiss me," she said. She ran her finger over the tip of his cock. "Guess where I want to kiss you."

Jack debated the downside of getting arrested for public indecency. The fact was, if she kept this up much longer, he was going to rip the damn skirt off and pull her down on top of him.

From her smile, she knew *exactly* how desperate he was.

Fortunately for Jack's career, the cab pulled to a stop in front of her building.

"We're here," Ronnie said, a sultry smile dancing on her lips. She opened her door and slid out, tossing him a saucy look. "Are you coming?"

He laughed. "Soon," he said. "Very, very soon."

chapter
seven

An all-night restaurant, the Prado Diner catered mostly to tourists and neighborhood locals. The atmosphere was laid-back, the tips were good, and Marina liked working the graveyard shift.

After work, she walked home as usual, exhausted but not willing to pay for a cab. It wasn't quite five, and delivery trucks were double-parked along the damp, newly swept streets. She waved at Bernie, the old man who owned the bakery at the corner. He smiled back, holding up a cheese Danish. Marina shook her head, laughing. Every day he offered, and every day she declined. One day, she was going to accept and rock his world.

She continued down the street, humming to herself, in a good mood despite her weariness. She'd peeked twice into her Kenneth Cole tote, just to make sure her purchase was still there, wrapped in brown paper and tucked next to a copy of *Vogue*. She couldn't wait to get home and set it on her coffee table—a real first edition, and of Henry Miller no less.

She pulled herself up a little taller, an added spring in her step. The sad truth was that although she'd been to several talks at Archer's Rare Books, she still felt a little decadent even *thinking* about stuff like that. So for her to have actually returned to the store the previous afternoon and bought it…well, that was the kind of step her therapist would surely call a breakthrough.

She'd never done anything like that back when she'd been dating Randy. They'd gone to pubs, had a few beers, and then had some wham-bam-thank-you-ma'am sex on the bed on top of the covers. Once, they'd done it on the floor. That had been the high point of Marina's sex life.

She'd wanted more. More of what, she didn't exactly know. But when Randy had gone and dumped her, Marina had resolved to figure it out. The lectures on erotica she'd seen advertised had seemed like a good place to start.

Considering she didn't have a current boyfriend, she wasn't entirely sure how her newfound familiarity with erotic literature would affect her sex life. She hoped to find out soon, though. In fact, Nat Archer had seemed like a prime candidate. He'd chatted with her at all three of his sister's lectures. Probably just professional courtesy, but Marina had to admit she liked the way he looked at her.

And she liked to remember that look on evenings when she was home alone with nothing but her thoughts and her books. So far, she'd been doing a lot of buying online and had amassed quite a collection of erotica, and she rather liked kicking back with a glass of red wine and a few pages of pure titillation. Tonight she'd pop in a movie, pour a glass of Chianti and skim her new purchase. Heaven.

She reached her apartment and tugged on the outer door, then stepped into the small foyer. Her mailbox was empty except for a catalog, a flyer and a preapproved credit application for a local furniture store. She tossed it all in the garbage and headed up the four flights of stairs to her apartment. She wasn't thrilled about living in a walk-up, but she did like the way the stairs kept her legs in shape. And the fact that it was rent-controlled made it all the better.

When she reached her door, she pulled out the spare key she kept meaning to return to its hiding place under the planter on the first floor. She'd lost her own key ring almost a month ago and still hadn't gotten around to getting all her replacements made.

She slipped the key into the dead bolt, frowning when she realized it wasn't engaged. Damn. At least twice a week she forgot to turn the bolt.

Annoyed at herself, she pushed inside, tossing her purse on the sofa as she headed for her tiny bedroom to change clothes. She clicked on the halogen lamp in the corner as she moved, casting the living room in a mix of light and shadows.

She'd made the bed that morning, stripping the dirty linens and remaking it in the sparkling white sheets she'd got on sale at Macy's. She'd even splurged on a brand-new duvet and matching pillow covers. And now the bed was the focal point of her small room, a rose-pink duvet and ruffled pink pillows looking all bright and ready for some action.

She ran her hand over the fabric, smoothing it. Humming, she went into the bathroom and washed her makeup off, first spreading cold cream, next filling the basin, then splashing the water on her skin thirty-five times. She grabbed a towel and blotted her skin dry, then let the towel hang around her neck as she headed back into the bedroom to rummage for her jammies.

A bit of white against the dusty pink caught her eye, and she frowned, her brain finally registering what it was—an off-white envelope, her name scrawled across it in formal calligraphy print, like a wedding invitation or something. But this was no invitation. Her heart skipped a beat as the full impact of the situation hit her—she hadn't laid anything on the bed, and it had been pristine just moments before.

Near frantic, she backed against the wall, her head going this way and that as she searched the room. Her hand reached to the side, grappling for the tiny ceramic jewel case on her dresser. Not much in the way of a weapon, but it was something.

"Hello?" she whispered, inching toward the doorway. She'd never paid to have a phone jack installed in the bedroom, and now she needed to either get out of the apartment or find the phone and dial 911.

No answer. Not that she'd really expected one.

She inched closer to the living room, calculating the time it would take to get to her door, throw the lock and race into the hallway. In the doorway, she took another quick look around. Nothing in the living room looked out of place.

The fire escape creaked, a large shadow passing outside the open window.

Open?

Marina screamed.

For years, Ronnie had been addicted to Diet Coke. But that was nothing compared to her addiction to this man. She couldn't get enough of him.

They'd made love in her entrance hall, barely able to close the door behind them before stripping off their clothes. He'd been rock hard, and it thrilled her to know she'd done that to him.

She'd felt decadent, touching him like that in the taxi. It had taken all her control not to forget where they were and straddle him, riding him hard as they bounced along in the cab.

After the hall, they'd had an encore encounter on the couch, then retreated to the bedroom and had a few more—three, to be exact—fabulous, wild encounters in her bed. And against the wall. And on her desk.

"A crash course," she'd whispered at one point. "There'll be a quiz in the morning." They'd finally drifted off to sleep, a tangled mess of body parts.

Now her alarm was blaring, and Ronnie scrambled to hit the button. She managed to shut off the noise, then scooted back against Jack. She was sore and tired and stiff…and so very ready for more.

"Jack?" She snuggled closer, her breasts pressed against his back, her hand reaching over him to stroke his bare chest. "Are you asleep?"

No answer.

She licked the edge of his ear. "Jack?"

"You're insatiable." This time his whispered response drifted to her. "Time to get up and start the day."

She laughed. "Meanie."

He growled in response, then flipped over. He maneuvered her, too, until she was spooned up against him, and his hand rested lightly above her belly button. "Rise and shine," he said, his voice low and by her ear. "Gotta go take a shower, get moving, get that blood pumping."

His hand drifted up, tracing lazy circles on her breasts.

"Exactly what kind of pumping did you have in mind," she murmured. "Because that's not going to get me out of bed."

"Sorry," he whispered. But he didn't stop. Instead he caught her nipple between two fingers, teasing and tugging until she was certain a wire was carrying sensations from her breast to the pulsing between her thighs.

She moaned, squirming slightly. "I thought you wanted to get up," she whispered.

"I do," he said. "Absolutely. Hop on out."

"You're not exactly making that easy."

"Sorry," he said, but his voice lacked an apologetic tone.

She smiled to herself, determined to show him, and she started to slide to the edge of the bed.

"Ah-ah," he said, moving his hand from her breast back

to her belly, just a warm pressure, but enough to keep her in place.

His touch alone turned her on, but when his fingers trailed down, finding her center, Ronnie groaned, a low sound of pure need.

His fingers urged her open, and he slipped one digit inside. She automatically opened her legs wider, wanting more of him. Hell, wanting all of him.

"I'm going to be late for work," she said.

"What?" he murmured. "I'm not worth it?"

"I take the Fifth," she said, then laughed.

"Woman, you wound me." He flipped her onto her back, straddling her. She laughed, squirming under him in mock protest, and realizing that she hadn't had this much fun—not to mention this much sex—in a very long time.

"Oh, no," he said. "There's no escape for you."

"No?"

"No."

She slid her hands along his back, urging him down. "Good," she said.

It was his turn to laugh. "We should get up, you know."

"Forget it," she said. "You're mine now."

"That," he assured her, "was my plan."

He kissed her, his tongue coaxing her lips open. She gave herself to him willingly, lifting her hips up in a silent urging for more. He slid into her, just a little, and she thought she was going to scream with frustration. But then he thrust again, burying himself completely inside her.

She rose up to meet him, sore and achy, but in absolute heaven. He made love to her slowly, compared to their earlier frantic coupling. A warm flush spread through her body, gathering between her thighs and then building and building until she was close. So close.

So very, very close.

Beep, beep, beep.

She jumped, startled, as he muttered a curse and slid off of her, rolling to the side. He fished around on the floor and came up with his pager.

She raised an eyebrow. "This is what I get for sleeping with a cop."

He laughed and cupped her sex. "No way, sweetheart. *This* is what you get for sleeping with a cop." He gestured with the other hand holding the pager. "This is what I get for not being an accountant."

He pressed a button and glanced at the readout. "I've got to go."

She nodded, disappointed but hardly in a position to argue. "Don't the criminals realize just how close I was?"

His mouth twitched. "Almost but not quite," he said.

She nodded. "Damn pager."

"I'll second that."

She flashed him a coy smile. "I suppose I could just finish on my own...."

"No way. I own that orgasm, and I'll be back to collect."

She sat up, laughing, the sheet falling around her waist. "A man who pays his debts," she said. "I like that."

And, even more, she liked Jack Parker. She sighed as a little tremor shook her body. She'd started out simply wanting a warm body in her bed, and she'd ended up with Jack.

Despite the utter lack of progress on the robbery, despite the sad state of her balance sheet, and despite her damn broken air conditioner, this week was definitely shaping up.

chapter
eight

"Another one," Donovan said as soon as Jack stepped into the lobby. "Only this time with a twist."

"A twist?" Jack asked. He followed Donovan up the four flights of stairs, past crime-scene techs and the tech from the coroner's office. *The coroner.* Jack clenched his fist. "Shit," he said "A homicide."

Martin Spinelli met them at the door. "That's right, Jack. Guess this one's no longer your turf."

Jack resisted the urge to tweak his little pig nose. Spinelli was a good cop with a bad attitude. On a good day, he rubbed Jack the wrong way. And while this had started out as a good day, it was rapidly disintegrating.

"Then why am I here?" he asked.

"Our guy's calling card," Donovan said. "It was on her bed."

"Looks like your little friend's moved up in the world," Spinelli added.

With Donovan at his heels, Jack stepped past Spinelli and entered the apartment. The smell of death hung in the air, a putrid stench of someone voiding their bowels. Not a particularly graceful way to go, but, then again, neither was murder.

A woman was sprawled on the floor, her skin already pallid. A large bruise had formed across her throat, and her eyes were open in a permanent expression of surprise.

Marina. The woman had been at Ronnie's lecture. And seeing her here, dead, didn't sit well.

He knelt beside her, his eyes meeting the tech's, who was busy working with the body. "Crushed windpipe?"

The tech, a young woman with curly red hair pulled back into a messy ponytail, nodded. "Looks that way." She gestured toward a brass candlestick tossed carelessly on the floor near the fire escape. "That looks to be the weapon. We'll check it for prints and trace evidence, but I'm not expecting any surprises."

Jack nodded and stood up, then crossed to the candlestick. He signaled for one of the crime-scene techs, then confirmed that the weapon's location had already been photographed and measured. Reassured, he took a handkerchief and picked it up, careful to touch it as little as possible. "Heavy," he said, voicing what he already knew.

"Probably just whacked her across the gullet," Donovan said.

"No doubt," Jack said. "But why?"

"Because he's a fucking nutcase," Spinelli said, wandering up behind.

"Could be your homicide doesn't have anything to do

with my stalker," Jack said. "Maybe a jealous boyfriend. Came home, saw a romantic note apparently from some-one else—"

"And he killed her in a fit of jealous rage?" Spinelli snorted. "And I've got a piece of the Brooklyn Bridge to sell you."

Jack just shrugged, keeping his expression blank. "Could be." He didn't believe it for a second, but he wasn't about to get shouldered out of this investigation simply because his perp had upped the ante.

Spinelli just shook his head. "Fine. You want to play it that way, you go right ahead. You work the stalker and I'll work the homicide." He pointed a finger at Jack. "But once our cases intertwine, I'm pulling rank. I'll call you in for support, but—"

"I know," Jack said. "You're homicide division and I'm sex crimes and never the twain shall meet." Damned ri-diculous bureaucracy. But at least he'd bought some time.

He headed toward the bedroom. "Prick," Donovan said, but under his breath. The note was still there on the bed, illuminated under the flash of a photographer's bulb.

Jack waited for him to finish, then slipped on a pair of latex gloves and picked up the note. He skimmed the words, nausea rising with every sentence. He knew these words. He'd heard them only days before. And so had Marina Stephenson.

Silently, he passed the note to Donovan. His partner took it, his eyes coursing over the page. "Steamy stuff," he said.

"Isn't it?" Jack said. "Henry Miller. *Tropic of Cancer.*"

Donovan lifted a brow. "This consultant of yours is a miracle worker," he said. "Already, you're an expert."

"She's good at what she does," Jack said, his voice noncommittal. "Let's get coffee," he said, heading back to the living room. He needed to talk to Donovan, and he wanted to do it without Spinelli looking over his shoulder. He dropped the note into an evidence bag and passed it to Spinelli on his way out the door.

"*My* case," Spinelli said with a wry grin. "Just you wait and see."

Jack ignored him, heading for the stairs.

Donovan huffed behind him. "Spinelli's an ass," he said. "But you don't really believe that shit, do you? That we've got two different perps?"

Jack shook his head. "Hell, no. It's the same perp. And he's getting dangerous."

Their vic was one of Ronnie's clients. Their perp was quoting Ronnie's lectures. And Ronnie's brother had been talking with the victim just two days before. Not necessarily damning. But from Jack's perspective, all of it was just a little too close to home.

Once they got back to the precinct, Jack filled Spinelli in on Marina Stephenson's identity. Spinelli played tough, and there was no denying the cases intertwined. But Jack was on the investigation, and it would take an act of God to get him off.

"I'll start tracking down the alibis of everyone else at that lecture," Spinelli said, conceding Jack's involvement. "Can your little expert get us a list?"

"I'll take care of it," Jack said.

"Suppose I should check her alibi, too."

Jack met his eyes. "Don't bother."

Spinelli half smiled, clearly understanding. "Last consultant I worked with was an accident reconstructionist. Heavyset guy. Face like a walrus." He shoved a hand into his pocket. "Some guys have all the luck."

"Clean living," Jack said.

Spinelli barked out a laugh, then turned to leave. "I'm going to go nudge the forensics guys. Page me when you've got that list."

As soon as Spinelli disappeared into the hallway, Jack picked up the phone. Ronnie answered, sounding thrilled to hear from him.

"I need a favor," he said. "There's been a murder. Marina Stephenson."

There was a pause, then she said, "Marina? From my lecture?"

"I'm afraid so."

"My God. She was killed? When? How?"

"Last night or this morning," Jack said. "We don't have many leads. I want to get a list of people who attended your lecture."

"You think one of my customers killed her?"

"I don't know," he said, answering honestly. "It's just a starting point." Another long silence. "Ronnie?" he prompted.

"I'm sorry. This is all kind of surreal."

"I know. I'm sorry I can't tell you more. Honestly, there's not much to tell. Can you help?"

"Of course," she said. "But I'm not sure how much help my list will be. I don't require people to sign in, and when they do, I only take first names. The only way I'd have a last name is if they signed up for our mailing list."

"Can you fax me what you've got?"

"Sure."

He gave her the fax number. "I'll see you tonight?"

"I'd like that," she said. They said goodbye, and he was about to hang up. "Jack?"

"Yes?"

"Should I be worried?"

"No," he said, his voice firm. "I'll see you later."

They hung up. Then Jack immediately called dispatch and arranged for a patrol officer to keep an eye on the store—and on Ronnie.

A full day at the store, and Ronnie hadn't sold even one book. At least yesterday she'd had one sale.

She shivered, remembering her single buyer. Marina Stephenson. Now deceased.

Ronnie sighed. The woman's check hadn't even cleared, and now she was dead. It just didn't seem real.

A quick rap at the door startled her, and she opened it to reveal Jack.

"Hey, beautiful," he said. "You doing okay?"

"Better now that you're here," she admitted. "It's been a strange day." She moved to him, sliding comfortably into his embrace. "Can we talk about it?" she asked.

He brushed a loose strand of hair away from her face. "Later. I promise." He lowered his mouth to hers and kissed her. Soft at first and then deep and probing, it was the kind of kiss designed to chase her worries away.

It worked, and her heart picked up its tempo. "What are we doing between now and later?" she asked, a little breathlessly. "Do you have something specific in mind?"

"Actually, I do." He reached back and pulled out the pencil she'd used to secure her hair in a loose bun atop her head. Her hair tumbled down, tickling the back of her neck. She held her breath as he ran his fingers through the strands. "Jack?" she finally prompted.

"Dinner," he said.

She blinked. "Dinner?" she repeated stupidly.

He dropped her hair and took a step backward. Ronnie kicked herself. He took a deep breath, and she held hers. Finally, he spoke. "Yes," he said. "I'd like to take you to dinner. I'd like to forget about everything else. Everything except you, me, food and wine." He tilted his head to the side, his endearing grin reflected in his eyes. "Miss Archer, would you do me the pleasure of joining me for dinner?"

Her heart fluttered, and she was certain she was grinning like an idiot. She took his outstretched hand and inclined her head, just so. "Why, thank you, Detective. It just so happens I'm free for dinner."

She'd gotten under his skin.

As he held the cab door open for her, Jack realized just how much Ronnie had wriggled her way into his heart without even trying. Maybe Jack had wanted to give women and relationships a wide berth until the Kelly fiasco had faded to a dim memory, but Veronica Archer had come crashing into his life, and he saw no reason to push her back out.

And, truth be told, now that Ronnie was in his life, Kelly *was* a dim memory. Hell, he could barely remember the color of her hair. Instead, he could only see Ronnie's dark waves, her vivid green eyes. She'd snuck up on him and smacked him upside the head. He felt like Wile E. Coyote, with stars and chirping birds spinning around his bewildered little brain.

He got in the cab after her and slammed the door shut, taking her hand. She was in his life now, and he intended to see that she stayed there.

When he'd finally called it a night, all he wanted to do was get to Ronnie's store. Not for his lesson. Not for sex. He just needed to see her again. Needed to see for himself that she was safe.

He wished he could believe it was just professional concern, but that was a load of crap. He'd fallen for this woman. He'd started out thinking with his dick, and damned if the rest of him hadn't followed suit.

He knew he should be asking her relevant questions about the case. About Marina Stephenson. About Henry Miller. About the fact that Nat's name hadn't been on the passenger list of any flight leaving New York that morning.

He told himself not to jump to conclusions. Nat could have decided to forgo flying and taken a train. Or his flight might have left from another state. Jack only had the preliminary results back from the airlines. It was way too early to start nailing down scenarios.

He remembered the robbery at Ronnie's store, and wondered if Nat was clever enough to fake a break-in to throw the scent off him. Jack pondered that for a minute, then wondered if he was giving the guy a fair shake or if his initial dislike of Ronnie's brother was coloring his perceptions.

Either way, right then, he didn't want to think about the case. Didn't want to consider that Ronnie's brother might be a killer. And he certainly didn't want to see the haunted look in her eyes when she learned that Nat was a suspect.

No, he just wanted to share a few hours with her. He wanted to clear his head, to enjoy their time before the demons of his job intruded.

"You're awfully quiet," Ronnie said. "Weak from hunger?"

"Something like that," he said with a laugh. The cab pulled up in front of J. Nouveau, a trendy little restaurant that had opened about a block from Jack's apartment. Not his usual sort of hangout, but it seemed perfect for a date.

"I'm impressed," Ronnie said. "It's impossible to get a table here."

Jack blanched. He hadn't actually considered that part of the equation. "Hold on," he said, then headed toward the door. A brief conversation with the maître d' yielded no good news, not even when Jack promised that New York's finest would keep an eye on the place. Damn.

He headed back to Ronnie, more than a little sheepish. "Would you believe me if I said I never intended to eat here? That I have someplace much more amazing in mind?"

A muscle in her cheek twitched, and he knew she was fighting back laughter. "I'd probably believe it," she said. "I'm pretty gullible."

"Lucky for me," he said. "Come on."

Two blocks and three flights of stairs later, they were in his little rathole of an apartment. Actually, the apartment itself wasn't bad, but the building was one of those that gave Manhattan apartments a bad name, thanks to a co-op board that couldn't manage to get its act together.

"*Zagat's* gives this place a great rating," Ronnie said.

"Careful," Jack said. "You'll be eating your words soon. I make a mean macaroni and cheese."

She laughed. "I stand corrected."

He exhaled, shoulders sagging. "I'm sorry. I haven't done the dating thing in a while, and it didn't even occur to me to make reservations. I just wanted..." He trailed off, not really sure what he meant to say.

"What?"

"Time," he said, the answer coming to him without thought. "I just wanted time with you."

Her smile turned sultry. "We had a lot of time last night," she said. "And the night before that. A nice time, too."

He cringed just a little, hoping he wasn't acting like an ass. They'd had some good times, and their little shopping excursion had been fun, but he had no real indication that she wanted anything other than sex, sex and more sex. He might be wanting to backtrack to first-date mode, but for all he knew, she wanted to get naked and go at it like bunnies.

Not that he was against that plan in principle...

"Jack?" Concern laced her voice.

He shook his thoughts away, then gestured toward the door. "We can still go out. There's a Thai place around the corner that hardly ever has a crowd. We could—"

"No. Thanks." She smiled at him, but this time there was nothing sultry about it. Just a real, honest smile. "I'm glad we're here. I was curious about where you lived."

He waved a hand, encompassing the tiny studio. "Voilà. It used to belong to a cousin. I sublet it a few years ago when he moved back home to Brooklyn. Hell of a lot easier than commuting." He shrugged. "The place went co-op, and I exercised Graham's option to buy. So it's all mine. All six-hundred-and-twenty-three square feet of it."

"I like it," she said. "It's cozy."

"Compared to your place, it's a closet."

She nodded. "I love that old place. It was my great-grandfather's and now it's mine."

He frowned. "And your brother's."

She shook her head, surprising him. "Not really. Nat's my half brother. Same mom, but different dad." She shrugged. "Daddy adopted Nat, but they never really got along. So I got the building."

"Nat was cut out?"

"He has his apartment," she said. "If I sell, Nat gets to either keep his apartment or the proceeds from the sale of his apartment. But it's not his decision whether or not to sell. So long as I don't sell, he can stay for life. But he can't pass it on. The whole place is mine to leave to my kids or grandkids or cats if I end up an old maid."

Jack took that in, wondering how Nat felt about that arrangement. "And he's okay with that?"

She shrugged. "It's a moot point, really, since we get along fine living on top of each other, and I'm never going to sell." A shadow passed over her face. "At least, I'm going to do my damnedest not to sell. Times are tight, but we should be able to squeeze by." She licked her lips. "So long as times don't *stay* tight."

"Nat's not involved with the store?" If Nat didn't know erotica, maybe Jack had focused on the wrong scumbag.

"He works there sometimes to help out, but his love was always pictures, never books. He started out in journalism, hoping to please our dad, then drifted into photojournalism. Now he's pretty much exclusive on the photo part." She cocked her head and smiled. "That's where he is now. On a shoot in the Galápagos Islands for *National Geographic*. Isn't that cool?"

She seemed so proud that he could hardly argue. Instead, he just nodded. "Amazing," he said, making a mental note to call the magazine.

"Since he travels so much, the strange terms of Daddy's will actually work out well for him. I mean, so long as I'm running the store, he's got a rent-free apartment. Considering housing costs, that's pretty good." She laughed. "Of course, that means that the air-conditioning is my responsibility."

"The perils of home ownership," he said. He pointed

toward his window unit. "Sears. Labor Day sale. Zero percent."

She laughed. "Detective, you really know how to romance a girl."

He laughed. "Come on, I'll give you the grand tour." She followed as he opened the door to the bathroom and the hall closet, then crossed diagonally to the kitchenette area. Being an observant woman, she immediately noticed the complete lack of cabinetry.

"You seem to be missing a large part of your kitchen," she said.

"My fatal flaw," he admitted. "I tinker." He always had. Woodworking helped him let off steam, and in Jack's line of work, a lot of steam could build up. Completely redoing his kitchen cabinets and enlarging the counter space should, if he was lucky, get him through this stalker-turned-murderer case without an ulcer.

"You know," he said, rethinking the prospect of cooking without counters. "There is always pizza."

She smiled. "And they deliver."

"Exactly." He held out his hand. "Let's finish the tour, and then we'll order." He grabbed the cell phone and led her to the couch, which, when pulled out, doubled as his bed. "The entertainment center."

She quirked an eyebrow, her thoughts obviously shifting to more prurient forms of entertainment. But he wasn't about to go there. Later, maybe. No, *definitely.*

Right now, though, he just wanted to be with her. To get to know her a little better. To have a *date,* even if he had managed to blow the dinner part of the equation.

He urged her down next to him, then hit the remote, scrolling through the channels until he found the movie choices. "What do you think?"

She shrugged. "Pizza, a movie and a man. What's there to think about?"

chapter
nine

There was, of course, a *lot* to think about. Like how much Ronnie wanted to simply snuggle close to this man. How much she wanted to feel his arms around her while she let all her worries about the store evaporate from her brain.

They were sitting together on the couch, so close their thighs touched, just holding hands. It was nice. She might have started out just wanting hot, sweaty sex with Jack Parker, but now she was perfectly fine just hanging out with him. Liked it, even. She felt a comfortableness with him, a relaxed quality, like with an old friend. Surprising in someone she'd known for so short a time, and yet somehow not surprising at all.

She'd clicked with Jack Parker. Even if he did prefer *The Matrix* to *Die Hard*.

On the television screen, Keanu Reeves bounced around, ducking bullets and leaping off buildings. She gestured with her half-eaten slice of pizza. "See, I just don't get that. I thought cops lived to watch movies like *Die Hard* and *Lethal Weapon*. You know, tough-guy films."

"You don't think this is tough?" he asked, gesturing to the screen.

She manufactured a snort. "The guy starred in *Bill & Ted's Excellent Adventure*," she said. "How tough can he be?"

Jack laughed. "We can turn the movie off," he said. "I can watch it anytime."

"Nah. I like it." She did, actually. "I'm just being difficult."

"Ah-ha," he said, laughing. "You're one of *those* women. High maintenance."

She shook her head in mock horror. "Never. Believe me," she said with what she hoped was a sultry grin. "It's very easy to keep me happy." She cocked her head. "So long as you study, you'll do just fine."

He squeezed her fingers. "I'm looking forward to a few all-nighters."

She took another bite of pizza and leaned against him, getting comfortable. "So what do you think of those movies?" she asked.

"Those movies?"

"Cop films. Are they like what you do?"

He laughed. "Not exactly. I hardly ever fire my gun except at target practice, and when I do fire it on the job, I get saddled with a small mountain of paperwork." He tapped the end of her nose. "Sorry to shatter your illusions."

"I'll never look at Bruce Willis the same way again,"

she said. She offered him her slice of pizza, and he took a bite. She smiled to herself, their easy familiarity making her feel cozy and intimate. "How'd you get into it?" she said. "Did you always want to be a cop?"

"Yup. My dad had thirty years on the force, and my grandpa was chief of police in a small town in Virginia."

"What about sex crimes? How'd you end up there?"

His face hardened. "Sex is a covenant. It's personal. I'm okay with anything between two consenting adults. But rape or child porn or any other shit that crosses the line…" He trailed off. The anger sparking off him was palpable. "People get hurt," he said, his voice low. "And it's my job to help make it better. At least a little."

She nodded, understanding. Someone *had* gotten hurt. For Jack, it was personal. "I'm sorry."

"I've always wanted to be a cop," he said. "For as long as I can remember." He met her eyes. "But I can pinpoint to the second the instant I knew I wanted to join the sex-crimes division."

His eyes burned with an intensity bordering on rage, and for a moment, she just held his hand.

"The family business," he finally said, clearly trying to lighten the mood. "It may not pay well, but at least I get to carry a gun."

She conjured a smile. "And a big one, too."

"How about you?" he asked.

She shook her head. "Never carried a gun."

He laughed, and she gave herself a couple of brownie points. "Is yours a family business?" he asked, prompting her.

"Sort of," she said. "The bookstore was my father's passion. And, don't get me wrong, I love it, too, but…"

"Your passion is the erotica," he said.

"Exactly." Ronnie nodded. "And it took me forever to figure that out." She shifted on the couch so she could see his eyes, then grinned. "When my dad ran the store, it carried nothing even remotely racy or erotic. I got into it because I wanted to shock my dad. I think I thought he'd consider it over-the-top, and then he'd pay more attention to me."

"Trying to rein you in."

"Right."

"Did it work?" he asked.

"Not at all," she said, a little bit surprised that she was revealing so much to him, but not inclined to stop. "Daddy couldn't have cared less. Nat seemed pretty interested, but he never really said anything to me." She raised an eyebrow. "Men."

He reached for another slice of pizza. "So I guess at some point you shifted from rebellion to serious interest?"

She nodded. "It's a fascinating subject. The way erotica ties in with the various cultures and with society's mores." She shrugged. "I don't have any interest in selling the bookstore. I grew up in that place—it holds countless memories. But I'm passionate about studying the erotica. That's why I'm getting my Ph.D. I'd like to teach it someday. And I definitely want to expand the store's collection."

He kissed her hand. "I'm passionate about you."

Her heart raced, her body shifting seamlessly from relaxed to primed and ready for action. "How you talk," she said, a tease in her voice.

He lifted his thumb and brushed it across her lips, the intimate gesture waking the butterflies in her stomach.

"Pizza sauce," he said.

"No doubt," she said.

"Thank you," he said.

She frowned, totally clueless. "For what?"

"For tonight. For this." He took her hand, his fingers tracing up and down between hers, the touch electrifying that entire half of her body. "Today was hell," he said. "And I wanted to see you." He cast about, as if searching for the right words. "I wanted...*this*," he said, waving his hand to encompass the room, pizza box and all. "A few moments of sanity. With you."

Her heart twisted. "Thank you," she whispered. She squeezed his hand. "Can you talk about it?" she asked. "Marina, I mean. Do you *want* to talk about it?"

Instead of answering, he got up and walked to the table near the door, then pulled a manila envelope out of his battered leather briefcase. He crossed back and handed her the envelope. She glanced up at him, then down. Silently, she peered inside. A single piece of paper.

"Go ahead," he said. "It's a photocopy."

Ronnie licked her lips and then grasped the paper gingerly between her thumb and forefinger, not certain she really wanted to see what it said. Her eyes scanned the page, bile rising in her throat. "That's the passage I discussed last night at the lecture."

"I know," he said.

"Coincidence?" she asked, even though she knew better. A stalker was out there, and now he'd begun to kill women. And he was using words *she'd* selected as his calling card. The whole situation gave her the creeps, and Detective Jack Parker was the only bright spot in what was turning into a very bad dream.

"I don't think so." He took her hand, his warm and reassuring.

"Someone at the lecture." A shiver racked her body, and she struggled to tamp down the fear.

"Probably," he said. "We're checking alibis." He turned to face her, his stance and manner professional. "Do you plan the lectures out ahead of time? Photocopy passages to review? Anything like that?"

She nodded. "Sure. My notes were probably sitting behind the counter or in the break room for at least a week. I'll scribble a thought here or there. Or stop and flip through a book and mark passages I might talk about."

"It could be someone who ran across your work."

"It could be my burglar."

He nodded. "Or even someone you know."

She pressed her lips together, then exhaled, but didn't say a word. The idea didn't sit easy.

He studied her, then clutched her hand. "It'll be okay," he said.

"How?"

He kissed her fingertips. "I don't like it, but you're mixed up in this. And I'm sticking to you like glue until we figure out why."

She nodded, reeling under the implications. A robbery. A stalker. A murder.

With a start, she remembered her admirer. "There's something else," she said. "I didn't mention it before because I didn't think my store had any connection to your case. But now..."

Concern etched Jack's face. "What?"

"It's probably nothing, but I've been getting little notes."

"Erotica?"

She shook her head quickly. "No. Clichéd stuff, actually. 'Sweets for the sweet.' That kind of thing." She shrugged, feeling a little silly as she revealed this. Surely her innocent little notes had no relation to the bold erotica left on women's pillows. Or the murder of her customer.

"Any ideas who your admirer is?" Jack asked.

"My guess is Tommy. The college kid who was at the lecture."

Jack nodded. "I remember him."

He didn't say anything else.

"Jack? Do you think they're related?"

"I don't know," he said. "Did you keep them?"

"I may still have one," she said, feeling cold. She'd expected him to laugh it off. Instead, he'd shifted into cop mode. "I'll check."

An involuntary shudder chased up her spine, and Jack gathered her in his arms, holding her close. They stayed like that for an eternity, Jack simply stroking her back and Ronnie breathing softly, trying to will the earth to quit spinning out of control.

After a moment, Jack squeezed her hand. "It's late and

it's dark and it's a fourteen-dollar cab ride to your place. I don't suppose I could interest you in staying the night?" He didn't mention that she probably didn't want to be alone in the dark, and she was grateful for the oversight.

She conjured a smile, then pressed the tip of her finger to her mouth. "Not a bad offer," she said. "But I don't have my jammies."

He trailed a fingertip up the side of her arm. "Sweetheart," he said, "you're not going to need them."

One thing was for certain—Jack Parker knew how to take Ronnie's mind off her fears.

His news of Marina's death had blindsided her, leaving her cold and hollow. Fortunately, Jack was there to warm her up. And warm her up, he did. They'd made love twice, both times slow and sweet. She'd drifted off to sleep safe in the circle of his arms, the bogeyman held at bay for at least a little longer.

The odd creaks and groans of the unfamiliar building had awakened her only moments before, and now she fumbled for her glasses and then squinted at Jack's digital clock—just past three in the morning and she was wide-awake.

Jack slept soundly beside her, managing to take up the majority of the bed. He'd stolen the covers, too, and when she'd awakened, she'd been pressed against him, seeking his heat to counteract the chill from his no-interest Sears special.

Now she climbed out of bed, careful not to wake him, and padded to the refrigerator. She'd intended to have some water, but the bottle of chardonnay tempted her, and she poured herself a glass. At the very least, the wine might help her go back to sleep.

The trouble with a studio, she soon realized, was that there was no place to go if she didn't want to wake Jack. Even though tomorrow—or, rather, today—was Sunday, she figured he'd be working. And from what she'd seen, the man hadn't gotten much rest lately.

With her wine clutched firmly in her hand, she padded barefoot to the window, stopping on the way to grab a T-shirt off the back of a chair and pull it on. She raised the blinds, glancing past the fire escape to the darkened courtyard beyond. Tilting her head back, she could see a smattering of stars.

She'd gone down to Texas once, to Archer City, where Larry McMurtry had opened several used and rare bookstores. An odd place, out in the middle of nowhere, but she'd enjoyed the trip and had made some fabulous purchases for the store. In Texas, there had been stars. Big sky. And at night, in the little town that shut down when the Dairy Queen closed, the stars had blanketed the heavens, as if someone had tossed diamond dust onto a thick spread of black velvet.

If she ever left Manhattan, Ronnie intended to live somewhere with a lot of sky. Now, though, she'd settle for just a little.

Careful not to wake Jack, she flipped the latch on the window lock and raised the sash. A flood of warm air rushed in, doing battle with the fabricated chill in the apartment.

The grated flooring of the fire escape felt rough against her bare feet, but she padded to the edge. Jack or someone had thrown a bamboo mat over the side, giving some privacy. A few hanging plants in desperate need of water hung from hooks attached to the flooring of the fire escape belonging to Jack's upstairs neighbor. Jack didn't seem the houseplant type, and Ronnie wondered about the dichotomy. Were they his, or were they remnants of a past relationship?

Breathing in the humid night air, she leaned up against the railing, most of her body hidden by the bamboo mat that formed a wall in front of her. As she glanced around, she sipped her wine, imagining she was Grace Kelly and Jack was Jimmy Stewart, and the only murders that touched her life were entirely fictionalized.

Not a bad fantasy.

Below her, the courtyard was dark, as were most of the apartments that faced inward toward the little patch of grass. A dim light burned behind the miniblinds of one apartment, but Ronnie couldn't see any sign of movement, and she guessed the occupant either slept with the light on, or was still out partying.

The floor shifted slightly, the metal structure creaking, and Ronnie started to turn. But then she felt the gentle pressure of Jack's hand on her shoulder.

"I woke up and you weren't there," he said. He swept her hair to one side and pressed a gentle kiss against her neck. An innocent touch, but it sent her body hurling into hyperdrive. As far as Ronnie could tell, it was physically impossible for her to get enough of Jack Parker.

His arms closed around her waist, and she shifted in his embrace just enough to see him. He'd pulled on sweatpants, but his chest was bare, and she reached up automatically, her fingers twining in the silky smattering of hair.

"Something woke me," she said. "I'm sorry if I made a noise. I didn't mean to disturb you."

"Impossible," he said. "You could never disturb me."

With a sigh, she faced forward again, leaning against him as his arms closed tight around her waist. She leaned back, her head tucked under his chin. Jack was a big man. Not Herculean, but big enough to make her feel safe in his embrace, and they stood together like that, the gentle thud of his heart working on her like a lullaby.

Her eyes were just beginning to droop when his hands shifted, grazing over the thin cotton of the T-shirt.

Her breath hitched in her throat, and she struggled to form words. "I was trying to make myself sleepy," she protested, but not very believably. "You're waking me up."

He nipped at her ear. "Sorry," he said, not sounding the least bit like he meant it. "But don't worry. Exercise is a great sleep aid."

"Oh?" she asked. "Are we going jogging?"

"No," he said, his hands gliding down with obvious purpose, over her breasts to the hem of the T-shirt. He pushed it upward, then pulled, tugging it over her head almost before she realized what was happening. "But I think I can promise complete and utter exhaustion," he added.

Her body responded immediately—her nipples tightening, the area between her thighs throbbing in anticipation. She stood there, utterly naked, only slightly hidden from the world by the thin bamboo mat, the angles of his fire escape and the leaves of one ill-watered fern.

"Jack," she whispered, a feeble protest.

"Sh." He pressed closer against her, and she could feel the stiff length of his erection jutting out against the thin fleece of his sweatpants. One hand stroked her belly, teasing dangerously low, while the other pulled at and played with her breast. A bone-deep heat spread through her body, and she idly wondered what would happen if she melted under his touch.

"This is our next lesson," he continued.

She frowned, fighting to make sense of his words through the haze of sensual pleasure that had hijacked her brain. No luck. "What?"

"Voyeurism," he said. "Exhibitionism. Aren't those staples of erotic literature?"

She recalled Bertha and the Monsieur. Was it only a few days ago she'd been reading about them, all alone with her fantasies?

"Uh-huh."

He slid his hand down, cupping her sex, his fingers gliding over slick heat. She gasped, a tremor shaking her body. "Tell me more," he said. With the tip of his tongue, he teased her ear. "Educate me."

Her body seemed to pulse, and Ronnie wasn't entirely certain her voice was going to cooperate, but she tried. "It…it is a staple. A very common theme." His finger slipped inside her, and she moaned, almost unconsciously shifting her stance to allow him better access.

"Public places?" he asked. "Secret trysts in parks and gardens?"

She swallowed, her skin tingling. "Sometimes." She forced the word out. "Sometimes private bedrooms with hidden peepholes."

"Tell me," he whispered. While that one finger teased her, his hand stroked lightly, up and down over her stomach, the edge of his finger grazing the underside of her breast on every pass.

She tilted her head back, resting against him, feeling decadent and wanton and so very turned on. "I was reading a story recently," she said. "Looking for dissertation material. *Voluptuous Confessions of a French Lady of Passion.*"

"Tell me about it," Jack whispered.

Ronnie shook her head, unable to form words.

Jack's low laugh tickled her ear. "Tell me, or I'll stop."

"No fair," she murmured, but she doubled her efforts to get her brain in gear. "The narrator is a young French girl, and she eavesdrops on her aunt and the aunt's fiancé." Her mind drifted back over the passage that had so engaged her attention only a few days before. "She's young, innocent. And she touches herself while she watches them make love."

Jack's hand continued to stroke, his lips brushing against the side of her neck. "What else?"

Ronnie swallowed, trying to focus. "Um, there's also *Fanny Hill*. And so many others."

"Do you think we're being watched?" Jack's whisper, low and dangerous, teased her senses.

She didn't think so. It was too late, the courtyard too dark, and the angle and obstructions on the fire escape too odd for anyone to have a clear view. Still, she had to admit a slight rush just from the possibility. "I don't know," she said.

"But we might be." He slipped another finger inside her, and she moaned, her body tightening around him. He slid in and out, building an erotic rhythm. Her knees turned weak, and she clutched the rail, almost afraid he'd stop if she changed her position, but it was either hold on to something solid or collapse to the ground.

He did stop, and she murmured a soft protest. But his cessation was brief, a quick break to shift his position so that his fingers could better stroke and tease her. "Spread your legs," he said. She complied, and his fingers found her clit, teasing her with a soft touch when she wanted to beg him for harder, faster, *more*.

He seemed to know, and as he pressed close behind her, his body hard against her back, his breath as fast as hers, he stroked her with definite purpose. Her entire body flushed warm as waves of pleasure ebbed and flowed through her, building toward one massive tidal wave of pleasure. Close, so very close.

"I want you to do something for me," Jack whispered.

Ronnie could only nod, pretty much willing to do anything he asked.

"Come for me," he said.

Ronnie groaned, his words stroking her as much as his fingers. And, like the polite woman she was, Ronnie happily complied.

The alarm clock buzzed at nine, and Jack slapped his hand down on the off button quickly before it woke Ronnie. As he pushed himself up, sliding his feet to the floor, every muscle in his body screamed in protest. He felt like he'd spent five solid hours working out at the gym.

Not a bad trade-off, actually. Have marathon sex, stay in shape.

Jack grinned, wondering how Ronnie would respond if he told her he wanted to keep her around so he could cancel his expensive gym membership. She'd probably laugh and tell him he'd have to be sure and compensate her well if she was going to be his personal trainer. That kind of compensation, Jack was more than happy to pay.

Even with the ache in his muscles, and despite the investigation weighing him down, overall he felt content. For that matter, he knew what people meant when they said they glowed. He was glowing, and the woman in his bed was why. Unexpected, lightning fast, but there you had it.

He shrugged, not particularly interested in psychoanalyzing himself, and got up to make coffee. She rolled over almost immediately, sprawling across the warm spot he'd left in the bed. She made a sleepy noise, rolled over again and buried her face in a pillow. Apparently his sleeping beauty wasn't a morning person.

Not that he could blame her. All told, they'd managed

maybe two hours of real sleep. Not that he was complaining…

He measured out the coffee, then filled the carafe, starting the water through the contraption. While the coffee-maker worked its magic, Jack headed for the bathroom, taking a quick shower and then throwing on a pair of jeans and an old NYPD T-shirt. He didn't mind working on Sundays, but he sure as hell wasn't wearing a tie.

He headed back across the room to the kitchen, then filled a travel mug with coffee. Mug in hand, he headed to the bed, then sat on the edge of the mattress. He touched her hair, and Ronnie brushed him away, as if shooing a gnat.

He grinned. Definitely not a morning person. He stroked her cheek. "Hey, sleepyhead."

She muttered something he didn't understand, then rolled over, cocooning herself in the covers.

He laughed and planted a kiss on her cheek. "Wake up, Ronnie. I've got to go."

That seemed to work, and she squinted at him. A slow smile spread across her face, and he resisted the urge to pull off his clothes and climb back into bed.

"Sorry to wake you, but do you need to get up? Or is the store closed today."

She pushed herself up to a sitting position, her brow furrowed in concentration. "Um, it's Sunday, right? We're open half a day. But Joan's working. I'm off. The store's closed Mondays and Tuesdays."

"Good," he said. "Stay here. You can go back on Wednesday, and in the meantime, we'll study."

She frowned. "Jack, I—"

"No argument," he said, plastering on his no-nonsense cop face. He wanted her close. Wanted to keep an eye on her. "The store's taken care of, your brother's out of town and you've got no air-conditioning."

She licked her lips, then nodded. "Fine." She glanced around, her gaze settling on the television. "I've got HBO, your sweatpants and leftover pizza. I'm good to go."

"I won't be late," he said, then bent over to kiss her on the nose. "Go back to sleep," he said. "Believe me, when I get home, you'll need your rest."

"When you get home," she said, snuggling back down under the covers, "you're taking me out to dinner. You owe me one dinner out."

"You're right," he said. He stopped in front of the door and shot her a grin. "Maybe I'll even make reservations."

"I'll believe it when I see it," she said, but her voice was already half lost to sleep.

He left quietly, pulling the door shut behind him. And as he twisted his key in the dead bolt, Jack realized he was humming a tuneless melody. He rolled his eyes and stopped, glancing around the foyer to see if anyone had noticed. He had no sense of rhythm and was utterly tone-deaf.

As a consequence, he *never* hummed.

But today Ronnie was waiting in his apartment for him to come home. And for Jack, that was reason enough to sing.

chapter
ten

"Page one," Donovan said. "Metro." He tossed the morning paper on Jack's desk.

"Any leaks?" Jack asked, thumbing through the newspaper.

"Nope. Clean as a whistle."

The night before, the investigative team had decided to withhold the information about the erotic note that had been found at the scene of Marina Stephenson's murder. A common enough tactic, the downside was that they might miss out on stalking victims who so far hadn't reported the crime, but might be scared enough to do so after reading about a murder.

"You still cool with the plan?" Donovan asked.

Jack nodded. "If we're at a dead end in a few days, I think we should leak it. But right now, I think this is the way to play it."

Donovan pointed at the ceiling, his eyes wide. "Look," he said. "There goes one."

Jack spun around, his gaze up, trying to find what his partner was pointing toward. "What?"

"A flying pig," Donovan said, managing to keep a straight face. "I knew when you and Spinelli finally agreed on something pigs would fly."

Spinelli lumbered over. "And monkeys will fly out of your butt, Donovan," he said. His gaze shifted from Donovan to Jack. "An accident," he said.

"Stephenson?" Jack asked, trying to keep track of the conversation.

"That's what the forensic guys tell me." He tossed a preliminary report onto Jack's desk. Jack skimmed it, then passed it to Donovan.

"So our stalker comes in and leaves his little present," Jack said, running through the scenario. "He's on his way out—"

"But Marina comes home," Donovan put in.

"Right," Jack said. "So our guy rushes to the fire escape, figuring he'll go down that way. But the ladder's gone."

"He panics," Spinelli said. "Rushes her."

"And when she screams, he grabs the handiest thing and swings it, wanting to shut her up."

The three men looked at one another. "Could be," Donovan said.

"It's still murder," Jack said.

Spinelli cracked a smile. "Which makes it my case."

Jack's phone rang and Spinelli turned away, chuckling to himself. Jack rolled his eyes and yanked up the handset. "Parker," he said, realizing it was a staffer from *National Geographic* who was returning his call.

The staffer knew nothing about the Galápagos shoot but gave him the home number of the editor who would have handled the assignment. The guy wasn't home, so Jack left his cell phone number and asked for a call back.

"Nothing on the brother?" Donovan asked.

"Nothing yet."

"Still think he's a suspect?"

Jack nodded. "Afraid so."

"Motive?"

"Don't have a clue. Scandal, maybe? Push Ronnie into selling the store?"

"Seems far-fetched," Donovan said.

Jack agreed. "Maybe we're simply dealing with a perv."

"Could be." Donovan kicked his feet up onto the desk. "So how are your lessons going?" he asked. "Does she know you're investigating her brother?"

Jack scowled. "You know me better than that. I'm not going to compromise an investigation by letting my suspect's sister in on my suspicions." And that was true no matter how hurt Ronnie was going to be when she found out. Jack only hoped she'd understand he had no choice.

"Makes sense," Donovan said. "And if you told her, your lessons might come to a screeching halt." His mouth twitched. "I mean, right now you're getting an in-depth and intimate look at the wild and woolly world of erotica. Am I right?" He squinted, his eyes filled with mirth. "What do they call those classes? Practicums?"

"You're a shit," Jack said.

"True," Donovan said. He shifted in the chair. "Seriously, how's it going?"

Jack wasn't sure if Donovan meant the consulting or the relationship. "Veronica Archer knows her stuff," he said simply.

"And?"

"And none of your business," Jack said. "I take it you've got nothing better to do than give me shit?"

Donovan laughed. "Actually, I've got news. I just got off the phone with Larry over in Brooklyn. He had a nice long talk with the lady over there who's been getting the deliveries."

"And?"

"And she participated in some online chat group thing where all these scholarly types gather to talk about erotica." He made a snorting noise. "Personally, I think they're just looking to get off."

"I wouldn't bet the ranch," Jack said, recalling the detailed bibliographic information in the bookstore's catalog. "Seems to me there's some pretty legitimate scholarly stuff going on."

He meant what he said, but Donovan just laughed. "Man, you've got it bad."

Jack scowled but didn't offer a denial. "We'll need to go talk to Caroline Crawley again," he said. "See if she's been in any similar chat groups."

Donovan nodded. "After that, you wanna grab some dinner? I thought maybe we could double-date. Cindy's got the night off. Have a drink, grab some dinner."

Jack cast him a sideways glance. "You're serious?"

"Shit, yeah. You gotta eat. And so does she. Especially if you two wanna keep up your energy," he added with a leer.

Jack rolled his eyes. "Tonight. Eight o'clock. The Turquoise Door. You in?"

"Oh, shit, man, you really got it bad. That's going to set you back a paycheck."

"You, too," Jack said. "Or are you going to take Cindy to the deli?"

Donovan scowled, but he caved. "You're on," he said. Jack hid a smile. Donovan didn't spend the kind of money the Turquoise Door required on just any woman. Something serious was brewing.

Then again, Jack didn't peel open his wallet on a regular basis for restaurants like that, either. He stood up, ignoring the implications.

"So you're coming?" he asked.

"Hell, yes," Donovan said. He met Jack's eyes one more time. "Dinner'll be a good time," he said. "And even if you won't admit it, it's all over your face. You're a lost cause, my man. You've fallen, and hard."

Jack didn't answer. Because, really, what could he do but agree?

For the fourth time, Ronnie picked the phone up, started to dial the precinct, and then slammed the handset back down. *Damn*.

She was going positively stir-crazy, and she desperately wanted to take a walk, go to a museum, buy a new pair of shoes. Anything to get her out of the apartment. But

Jack hadn't left her a key, and she had no way of locking up behind herself. Which meant she had two choices— stuck or irresponsible.

Irresponsible tempted, but in the end, she went with stuck.

Once again, she eyed the phone. She could just call him and ask if he had a key hidden, but she should have asked earlier when he'd called to ask her about getting her customer list. Now she hated to bug him and, even more, she was afraid he'd tell her he didn't want her going outside. She didn't want to hear him say that he thought she was in danger. So far, he hadn't said so, and she hoped that was because it wasn't true, that her imagination was just running away with her. But that didn't change the creepy feeling.

Flopping back down on his couch, she grabbed the remote and started flipping channels. Tonight, she'd make him take her by her place. She didn't mind staying another few days with Jack—she liked the thought, actually—but if she was going to be hanging around, she'd need fresh clothes. Also she wanted to be productive. At the very least, she could pick up a few reference books and her laptop.

There wasn't a thing she wanted to watch on any of the movie channels, so she clicked the television back off and picked up the phone. The juice on her cell phone had long since run out, but she could still check her messages. She dialed, then punched in the numbers for her password.

Seven new messages. She smiled. Always nice to be loved.

The first was a hang-up, and her little love fest faded a tad. The second was Nat, saying he was at his hotel and he'd call again later. After that, Ethan had called, wanting to discuss the wiring and her "utterly inadequate" breaker box. Joan called next, leaving an innocuous "call me" message. Another call from Ethan, saying he hadn't heard back and was afraid she hadn't received his first message. And the last from Nat, this time sounding a little pissed off.

Family first. She dialed Nat's cell phone number and left a message apologizing that she'd let her phone's battery run dry. Since she doubted there was cellular service in the Galápagos, she didn't know if he'd check his voice mail. But since he hadn't left a number, she had no other way to reach him.

She left the number for Jack's apartment and told him to try her there. She cringed when she said it. Considering their last encounter, she doubted her brother would approve of her temporary living arrangements.

Well, too bad for him. She could handle Nat. What she couldn't handle at the moment was being alone in her apartment, not with the break-in and this weird stalker stuff.

She grabbed a soda from the fridge, and then settled back on the couch, this time dialing the store.

Joan answered on the first ring. "Archer's Rare Books. How may I help you?"

"It's me," Ronnie said. "What's up?"

"Thank goodness you called," Joan said. "Ethan's been bugging me every half hour, wondering where you are."

Ronnie rolled her eyes. "Why do I need to be there so he can work up an estimate?"

"I don't know. But he seems to want to talk to you."

Ronnie sighed. "Put him on."

"I can't. He's gone now. He went to grab some lunch."

"Then tell him to do whatever's best for the store and my bank account." She drummed her fingers on her knees, wondering how much to tell Joan. "Anything odd happen today?"

"Not a thing. And thank goodness. I got the customer list pulled for the cops like you asked." She paused. "This whole thing is way too creepy."

"I know. Do you want me to come in?"

"No, I'm fine. Ethan will be back soon, and the patrol cops have stopped by twice already."

"You're sure?" Under the circumstances, Ronnie felt a little weird leaving her friend alone with a guy. But she'd told Jack about the electrical work—heck, he'd witnessed the air-conditioning problem firsthand. He'd expedited a background check on Ethan, and the electrician had passed with flying colors.

Not only did Ethan not have so much as a parking ticket, he was his high school valedictorian, and he took care of his invalid mother. An all-around nice guy, if overly shy. Apparently he knew it, too. Jack said the investigation had revealed that Ethan was taking a Learning Annex class in assertiveness. So far, Ronnie didn't think Ethan was getting his money's worth. Just to be on the safe side, Jack had also checked out Ethan's alibi. All clear.

Ronnie had been relieved. It was hard enough finding

an honest electrician. If hers had turned out to be a murderer, she didn't know what she'd have done.

"I'm *fine*," Joan insisted. "Are we still laying out the catalog on Tuesday? I need the bucks."

"Absolutely."

Joan cleared her throat. "Um, about those bucks," she said. "The store's doing okay, right? I mean, you're not going to have to let me go or anything, are you?"

Ronnie closed her eyes, not wanting to have this conversation, either. "You know I'd only do that if I was hanging on by my fingernails."

"I know. I guess that's what I'm asking. I know it's tight. And now with all this…"

"We're okay for now," Ronnie said. "It *is* tight, but I'm hoping it'll pick up. And I'd give you at least a month's notice, too." Even if that meant digging into her personal savings account to pay Joan's salary.

"I'm trying to help," Joan said. "But nothing I do seems to get the store any attention." Her words were harsh, with an edge that startled Ronnie. "It's so damn annoying."

Ronnie almost laughed, picturing Joan slamming her fist against the glass case, her perky little face screwed up with frustration.

"What are you trying now?" A month or so ago, Joan had hired her cousin to wear a sandwich board and walk the street in front of the store. Creative, but hardly the kind of advertising that drew the typical antiquarian book customer.

Joan exhaled loudly. "It doesn't matter. It didn't work. No biggie." Her voice was rushed, as if she wished she hadn't brought it up in the first place. "Listen," she said. "I have to go. Someone just came in. Maybe he'll buy us out."

She clicked off before Ronnie had a chance to say good-bye. Ronnie shrugged, staring at the phone, feeling a little irritated and oddly hollow. *Bored.* She was stuck in Jack's apartment, and her lifeline to the outside world had just hung up on her.

With a scowl, she clicked the television back on. Still nothing, and so she settled on a rerun of *Match Game* on the Game Show channel, a testament to the depths of her boredom. Jack's phone rang, and she snatched it up, happy to have even a telemarketer to talk to— *Why, yes, we would like some aluminum siding. The house in the Hamptons is in dire need of a face-lift.*

"Parker residence."

"Shit, Ronnie," Nat said. "I knew this had to be his number. What? Have you gone and moved in with the guy?"

She frowned at the phone. *Match Game* was looking better and better. "I'm just hanging out here," she said. "It's better than staying in the sauna I call an apartment."

"Is that the only reason?" he asked.

She wasn't entirely sure how to answer that. True, she had a rather open relationship with her brother, but *"No, the sex is a big incentive, too,"* didn't really seem like an appropriate response. She settled on avoidance tactics. "What do you mean?"

"The woman who died," he said, and something in his tone turned her blood to ice water. "She's one of your customers, right?"

Ronnie sucked in a breath. "How the hell did you hear about that?"

"I read, Ronnie."

She frowned. "It made the news in the Galápagos Islands?" *That* was surprising.

"I'm in Miami," he said, the irritation clear in his voice. "Late flight. Missed my connection. I'm stuck here until tonight and I picked up a copy of the *Times*."

"She is—*was*—a customer," Ronnie said. "She was even at the lecture."

"I thought so," Nat said. "I talked with her for a little bit. Nice lady."

"Nat?"

"What?"

She shook her head. "Nothing." She'd intended to ask him about the hard edge in his voice, but she could guess. His reaction was the same as Jack's—Ronnie's life had intersected with a murdered woman's. And that couldn't be good.

"Is that all?" Nat asked.

Ronnie blinked, not understanding the question. "All what?"

He released an exasperated sigh. "The article just said she was murdered. Did your detective friend tell you any more? There are always details they don't release to the press."

"Oh." She frowned. "Did the article mention the letter?"

"No." She could hear the exasperation in his voice. "What letter?"

She explained, and he sighed heavily. "Damn it, Ronnie. You're neck-deep in this. Close the damn store. You've got a master's. Go teach. Why the hell do you want to run a store, anyway?"

"Nat, I swear if you don't give it a rest…"

"Fine." The silence hung heavy between them, and she could picture his jaw grinding in that way he had. "I'm sorry," he finally said. "I just worry. I should never have left town."

She rolled her eyes. "I'm *fine.*"

"You're my little sister, and I worry about you."

Her mouth curved into a smile. He could be a pain, but she did love him. "I know you do. But there's nothing to worry about. Go on your trip, take wonderful pictures and drop me a postcard or two. Okay?"

"Okay." They chatted a few more minutes about nothing much, and then hung up. A feeling of unease settled over her, but she shook it off, chalking it up to boredom.

She glanced at her watch. Just barely past lunchtime. Probably hours before Jack got back. She drummed her fingers on her thigh, then clicked the television back on. According to the on-screen guide, if she switched channels every few hours, she could actually manage to watch four full hours of *Law & Order.*

She told herself it was educational. After all, if this thing with Jack continued, she'd need to be able to speak his language.

That seemed as good an excuse as any, and she settled back, Jack's scent on the sheets and his job—albeit fictionalized—on the screen in front of her.

* * *

Caroline Crawley didn't look too excited about having yet another interview with two men carrying badges. Not that Jack intended to let that stop him. She'd been the victim, true, but he needed information. And in light of Marina's death, Jack's investigation took precedence over minor inconveniences.

She led Jack and Donovan through the penthouse apartment to the patio overlooking Central Park. She'd been just settling down to lunch, and the housekeeper obligingly added two extra glasses of tea. If the stench of bourbon was any indication, Caroline was indulging in the tea only because she had company present. Jack almost told her to go ahead and have her whiskey, but he tamped down the urge.

She turned in her seat, her head perfectly straight, a slight glaze in her eyes the only hint that she'd been drinking. "What can I do for you, gentlemen?" she asked, directing the question at both Jack and Donovan.

"Have you had any other incidents?" Donovan asked.

She shook her head. "No. Thank God." She tapped out a cigarette from a pack, her hand shaking as she lit it with a small gold lighter she fished from a pocket. "My husband's tightened the security here. You'd think it was Fort Knox." She aimed a pointed glance at him down her nose. "Not that I'm complaining. I might not stay in this apartment otherwise."

Her voice and tone suggested cool composure. Only the slight cloud in her eyes and the contents of her drink suggested that her controlled demeanor was little more than a facade.

"I'm not sure what else I can do," she said. "I've already given several statements."

Jack nodded. He'd read them all. "Mrs. Crawley, do you study erotica? Collect it, perhaps?" He had a hunch this prim-and-proper woman would never admit to something so base as actually reading the stuff.

She stiffened. "This…*stuff*…has ended up in my apartment three times. And three times I've given a statement. And each time the investigator has asked me precisely that." She swallowed a gulp of bourbon. "My answer has never wavered."

Jack stifled a sigh. He'd hoped this would be easier. "Mrs. Crawley," he said, his voice as gentle as possible, "your husband was present for each of your previous interviews. But he's not here now, and I need the truth."

He met her eyes, knowing he was running the risk that she'd kick him out and call his supervisor. But he was right. In his gut, he was sure.

"It's important," he added. "A victim in Brooklyn mentioned that she participated in online chat rooms. The participants discussed erotica. Have you ever gone to one of those chat rooms?"

At first he thought she was going to simply ignore his question. But then she jammed her cigarette into the ceramic ashtray. "Not a chat room," she said. "An e-mail list." She looked up, her eyes defiant. "I'm interested in the subject matter. Carson wouldn't approve and so I didn't tell him. But I certainly don't think that gives some pervert license to enter my home and leave his little presents for me."

"No one is saying that," Donovan said.

She seemed to calm down a bit. She picked up the tumbler, swirling it slightly so that the ice tinkled against the glass.

"So what kind of e-mail list?" Donovan asked.

"It's like a community," she said. "You send your e-mail to one address, and your message gets broadcast to the group of subscribers to the list. I thoroughly enjoyed it, though there were many people on the list who had a much more intellectual understanding of erotica than I do."

She tapped out a fresh cigarette, lit it, then took a long drag. She exhaled, her mouth curving into the hint of a smile. "And, of course, there were a lot of assholes who were just there for the titillation factor." She chuckled. "Poor them. It really was a pretty scholarly list."

"Would you have access to the identity of the other participants on the list?"

She glanced down at her hands. "No."

Jack bit back a frown, certain she was either lying or withholding something. "Mrs. Crawley, it's important."

Her lips disappeared into a thin line. After a minute, her chin lifted. "Detectives, I've been married for thirty years. My husband is never home. My life can be…dull. If I corresponded with someone by e-mail—someone who said the right things and knew how to make me feel good—then I don't believe I should be made to feel guilty."

Jack clenched his fists. "Are you telling us that you had an e-mail relationship with someone you met on an erotica list and you neglected to mention that when you started finding bits and pieces of erotica in your house?" His voice was rising, but he couldn't help it.

Her eyes widened. "Oh, no. It's not what you think. He could never do that to me. We genuinely cared for each other," she said, and Jack realized she truly believed it. "He's wonderful."

Jack stifled a sigh, his eyes meeting Donovan's. "We'll need his e-mail address."

She shook her head. "I don't have it. Truly. I only replied to his e-mails, and I deleted everything right away. Carson doesn't use my computer very often, but…" She trailed off with a shrug.

"And the other e-mails you've received from the list?"

"Deleted, too, I'm afraid."

"A tech guy might be able to salvage something from the hard drive," Donovan said. "We'll need your computer."

Caroline shifted slightly, hesitating just a little too long.

"We could easily get a warrant," Donovan added.

"It's a laptop," she said. "You can take it with you."

"Do you have any idea about how we could get a list of all the e-mail addresses that subscribed to this list?"

She shrugged. "Even if you could, I doubt it would be much help."

"Why not?" Jack asked.

Caroline shrugged. "I could hardly use my regular e-mail address," she said. "So I went to one of those free sites and set one up. It's easy. They don't verify who you are. To the list, I was StarryEyes. And even the e-mail service didn't know my real name. I just made one up. I imagine most everyone else did, too."

Jack frowned. So much for that being a good lead.

"Everyone might not be as smart as you," Donovan said. "It can't hurt to take a look at the membership."

Jack nodded. Donovan had a point. "Mrs. Crawley, who runs the list?"

"A local store," Caroline said. "Archer's Rare Books and Manuscripts."

chapter
eleven

As soon as Jack stepped off the elevator at the precinct, Spinelli barked at him to come over. "What the fuck do you think you're doing?" Spinelli asked in a stage whisper as Jack approached his desk.

"What the fuck are you talking about?" Jack retorted.

Spinelli pointed toward the phone, his neck and face turning red. If Jack hadn't seen it a hundred times before, he would have feared Spinelli was having a heart attack. "I just got a call from some reporter. Said he'd gotten a tip that our killer was leaving little bits of erotica around town. You want to tell me how that leaked?"

"It sure as hell didn't come from me," Jack said, anger rising. "I'm trying to solve this case, not fuck it up."

He locked eyes with Spinelli, his blood boiling from the accusation.

But then the other man blinked, sagging down in his

chair. "Shit, Jack. This case is eating my lunch. And now we've got some asshole making fools of us."

"It wasn't a cop," Jack said.

"Your loyalty is touching. But if it wasn't a cop, then who the hell was it?"

"Coroner's office, crime-scene tech, a neighbor who overheard something." Jack paused, his eyes meeting Spinelli's. "The killer."

As the other cop digested that, Jack pulled out a chair and sat down. "What do you know about e-mail lists?" he asked.

Spinelli didn't even blink at the change in subject. "Not much," he said, his tone tempered with a hint of interest. "Why?"

While Jack ran down the information he'd received from Caroline Crawley, Spinelli kicked his feet up on the desk, looking bored. Jack knew better.

There were times when the senior detective could be a real prick, but Spinelli was a good cop, and Jack trusted his judgment.

Spinelli made a steeple out of his fingers and used it to prop up his chin. "So you think Marina Stephenson may show up on that e-mail list."

"That's my hunch."

Spinelli smiled. "If you're right, you're just edging yourself out of this investigation."

Jack nodded. "If Marina's on the list, then we've got a stalker with a homicidal bent. Either way, I'm working this case."

"Ah, what the hell," Spinelli said. The grin was back.

"I'll keep you in the loop. Us guys from homicide don't know erotica from a Marvel comic book," he added, affecting a backwoods drawl.

Jack rolled his eyes. "I'll ask Ronnie about the e-mail list when I see her tonight."

"Your per diem covers taking consultants to dinner?"

Jack didn't answer.

The other detective raised his hands. "Hey, whatever. Although you may be on thin ice, Parker."

Jack stiffened. "How so?"

Spinelli shrugged. "She's knee-deep already, and yet no one's sending her naughty notes. That alone should put a big *S* on her forehead."

"She's not a suspect," Jack said, bristling.

"You don't think so?" Spinelli sounded genuinely curious.

"I thought about it," he admitted. "But no, I don't," he said, hoping that what he believed as a man lined up with what he should believe as a cop. "There's not a lot of scholarly sources for erotica in this town. Porn, yes. And outlets to buy erotica, absolutely. But resources for serious study? There just aren't that many."

"So the same thing that makes your girl a good consultant also puts her in the middle of this."

Jack nodded. "That's my hunch."

"Always go with your hunches," Spinelli said. "A cop's first line of defense." He grabbed the handset for his phone, silently signaling that they were done.

Jack headed out toward the elevator, thinking about Spinelli's words of wisdom. Usually he would agree. But where Ronnie was concerned, he was afraid that when his dick was engaged, his brain was turned off.

Could she be involved? Spinelli had seemed to think Jack's rationale made sense. Plus, Jack knew Ronnie. At least, he thought he did.

No. Ronnie wasn't a killer. Hell, he felt disloyal entertaining the thought even for an instant. He reminded himself that he was only doing his job, considering all possibilities. And that included Ronnie.

But his gut told him she wasn't involved—other than having stumbled into the middle of a pervert's erotic wet dream. And he trusted his gut. His real fear wasn't that she was a killer, but that her brother was. And as Jack got closer, was he putting Ronnie in line to be the next victim?

The thought made him quicken his step. He wanted to get home. To see her. To know she was safe.

The truth was that he had no proof Nat was involved. None at all.

In reality, he knew only two things for certain. He'd fallen hard for Veronica Archer. And she was getting mired deeper and deeper in whatever the hell was going on.

And Jack didn't like that. He didn't like it one little bit.

Detective Donovan was a big man who looked like his usual dinner consisted of a Swanson's Hungry Man meal or a Big Mac with fries and a shake. He was coarse and brash and, from what Ronnie could tell, totally smitten with the petite blonde sitting next to him.

Ronnie had liked him instantly.

"I mean, what is this shit?" Donovan said, staring at the plate the waiter had slid in front of him.

"Dinner," Jack said, the corner of his mouth twitching.

"This stuff's supposed to keep me alive?" He poked at his dinner with the tip of his fork. Two tiny beef medallions, two asparagus spears and two little mounds of garlic-whipped potatoes. All arranged quite elegantly on the plate. "There's nothing here. A man could starve to death, and pay mightily for the privilege."

Ronnie took a bite of bread, not because she was hungry, but to keep from laughing.

"I've got a chocolate cake at home," Cindy said. "Don't worry, I won't let you starve." The nurse flashed Ronnie a conspiratorial smile. "Believe me, it's in my best interest to make sure you aren't weak from hunger."

"Damn straight," Donovan said gruffly. But when he looked at Cindy, all irritation faded from his eyes, replaced by a genuine sparkle of affection.

Under the table, Jack squeezed her hand. Ronnie squeezed back, cherishing the gesture. He'd been sweet enough when he'd come home, but he hadn't talked about the case at all, and he seemed distant. She even thought she sensed guilt or embarrassment or some other emotion that made no sense.

She'd told herself she was imagining things, that she didn't know him well enough to read his moods. And that this was probably simply the way he was after a long day at the office. She told herself that over and over.

But she didn't actually believe it.

He'd been polite and cheerful on the surface all through

dinner, but still something was missing. And now, when he squeezed her hand in that familiar way, her eyes brimmed with tears, and she realized just how worried and frustrated she'd been by his standoffish behavior.

She pushed her chair back, putting her napkin on the table as she stood up. "Excuse me," she said. "I need to run to the ladies' room."

She didn't, of course, but she was afraid she'd do something silly like break down in tears. And then she'd have to make up an excuse or fess up and tell Jack that she'd fallen for him so hard that one slightly bad day on his part made her all insecure and needy.

Pathetic.

He caught up with her in the corridor by the restrooms.

"Hey," he said, taking her elbow, "are you okay?"

She nodded, fighting tears once again. This time not because he was pulling away from her, but because he'd actually noticed. Apparently, she was wired to cry at both the good and the bad. Either she was falling in love or she had PMS.

She flashed him a wavering smile. "I'm fine. I'm sorry."

"No, I'm sorry. I've been behaving like a jerk."

She shook her head. "No, you haven't. You had a rough day. Why should you have to come home and act all cheerful just because I'm there?"

"You're the reason I want to be cheerful," he said. "You're also the reason I feel like the world is pressing down around my shoulders." He drew in a deep breath, then took her hand. "I know you're not involved," he said. "I want you to believe that."

For a second, she didn't know what he meant. And then her eyes widened. "In the murder? My God, of course I'm not."

"I *know*," he said. "But…"

She understood. All of a sudden the evening made sense. "But you thought about it," she said. "For a minute or so, you wondered if I wasn't pulling some sort of *Basic Instinct* thing."

His sheepish expression was answer enough.

Rising up on her tiptoes, she kissed his cheek. "It's okay, Jack. You're a cop. It's what you do. And I'm not stupid. I don't know how or why, but somehow this thing keeps bumping up against me." She licked her lips, hating the truth of what she was saying. "Maybe one of my customers is a psycho. Maybe he stole my notes. I don't know. But we both know I'm involved somehow." She tilted her head sideways. "But not *like that.*"

He pulled her into his embrace, and the band around her heart loosened as he squeezed her tight. "I'm sorry."

"Don't be." She pulled back, just enough so that she could see his eyes. "You don't still think so, right?"

"I *never* thought so," he said. "It was just one of those horrible ideas that pop into your head." He traced the line of her jaw with his fingertip. "There's another horrible idea, too. And my fear is that I'm right about this one."

She scowled, this time not sure what he meant. She shook her head, signaling her confusion.

"I don't want anything to happen to you," he said simply.

She ran her teeth over her lower lip, understanding dawning. "I guess you'll just have to stick close to me," she said, trying not to let him know just how scared she was. He was worried enough without adding her fears to his.

"That's my plan," he said. "Come on," he said, taking her hand and urging her toward the table. "This is supposed to be a dinner date. We're not on the clock."

She tugged him back. "You don't have to pretend you can turn the cop part of you on and off. I know better than that."

His eyes held hers for a minute, and then he nodded. "Okay. I need to see who subscribes to your e-mail list."

"Wow. You really are in cop mode, aren't you?"

For half a second, he looked uncomfortable, and she put a reassuring hand on his arm.

"I'm teasing," she said. "Of course I'll get you the list. We can go right after dinner."

"Thanks."

She met his grin. "No problem. Anything I can do to help. Like you said, it's my ass on the line."

"I don't think I said it quite like that," he said. "But you're right. And for the record, it's a hell of a nice ass."

"This is it," Ronnie said, pointing to the screen of her laptop. "But I'm not sure how useful it will be to you."

She'd downloaded a list of e-mail addresses to a text file, and now she clicked the print button. A printer on the far side of the room started whirring.

"So this is just for scholarly stuff?" Jack asked.

"That's the intent," she said. "Although I get the occasional nutcase subscribing to the list."

"What do you mean?"

"You know. Creepy stuff. Like how he wants me and how my breasts are lush and how I'm his flower, pure and opening up just for him." She shuddered. "That was the one that really grossed me out."

Jack itched to slug the bastard. "Do you know who?"

She shook her head. "Weird e-mail addresses. I block one, and a new one pops up."

"Same guy."

"I don't have any way to prove it, but yeah." She shrugged. "He was the worst, but my list attracts a lot of weirdos. Nature of the beast, I guess."

Jack nodded. She was probably right.

The printer spit out a piece of paper, and Jack grabbed it.

"It'll show the blocked ones, too," she said. "But I doubt they're helpful."

Unfortunately, she was right. Just as Caroline Crawley had anticipated, most of the e-mail addresses made little sense, and most were from free services such as Yahoo! and Hotmail, which meant that if the subscriber used a fake name, it would be nearly impossible to trace back to them.

He skimmed the list and one address jumped out at him. "Well, damn," he said. "Check it out." He showed the page to Ronnie.

"Msteph," she said. She met his eyes. "That was probably Marina."

"Can you e-mail the list to our computer guys?"

"Sure. You'll want to let them look back at all the old messages," she said, typing the information into an e-mail. "They can call me if they have questions, but I've included my password and stuff. They should know what to do. It's pretty simple."

Jack gave her the e-mail address, added a note, then watched her press Send. A little bit of progress, he supposed, but he wasn't encouraged. He had a feeling they were about to hit another dead end. The odds were good the killer was on the e-mail list, but not so good they'd find him by that route.

Jack forced himself to mentally pull back, keeping his mind open to the possibility that Nat wasn't his bad guy. Hell, in truth he'd welcome that solution. An anonymous bad guy they could catch and put away with no harm to Ronnie—emotional or physical.

He didn't know who the killer was. All he knew was it wasn't going to be easy to figure it out. Instead of looking for who, they should probably focus on why. And as for that, Jack had no ideas.

Frustrated, he rubbed his temples. "How about another lesson?" he finally said.

She raised a brow. "A real lesson? Or is this a euphemism?"

He laughed, then planted a quick kiss on her cheek. "Euphemisms later," he said. "Right now, I need to try to

get in this guy's head, figure out why he does this stuff."
He shrugged. "That's the only place I can think of to start."

The trouble with real lessons, Jack soon realized, was
that with Ronnie as the teacher, they turned him on as
much as their private lessons had. After an hour of sitting
across from her at the kitchen table going over Harris's
My Life and Loves and running through a brief overview
of Havelock Ellis, Jack was hard as a rock and not thinking about work.

He took her hand across the table. "We could take a
quick break."

Amusement danced in her eyes. "Slacker," she said. But
he could see her nipples peak under her T-shirt, and he
was certain she wouldn't protest too much if he pressed
the point.

"It helps with concentration," he said. "Gets the blood
flowing."

"For studying, you need blood to your *brain*," she said.
She got up and went to her refrigerator, then refilled her
glass of chardonnay. She sauntered back toward him,
then rested her hip against the edge of the table, looking down at him with a gleam in her eye. "Oh, I forgot.
You're a guy. Guys *do* think with their—"

"Now, now," he said, taking her hand and tugging her
close. Wine sloshed over the side of her glass, and she
laughed. She took a sip, then snuggled down onto his lap,
her kiss sweetened by the wine.

"I hold to my theory," she said. "And since you do need

to work, maybe we should take a little break and get some blood flowing to your, uh, thinking regions."

His thinking regions thought that was a fine idea, as did the rest of him, and he shifted her on his lap, sliding his arm under her legs so he could stand up and carry her to the bedroom.

On the bed, she immediately sat up, taking his hands and tugging him down to the mattress. Then she rolled over and straddled him, her knees on either side of his waist and her hands on his shoulders.

"Stay still," she said, her voice playful.

"Staying still wasn't exactly part of my plan," he said. "I was anticipating quite a bit of movement, actually."

"Nope," she said. Her fingers danced over the buttons of his shirt, opening, then pushing the material away. The room was hot, the ceiling fan doing little to combat the high temperature, and now the slight breeze felt cool against his sweat-dampened skin.

She pressed a kiss to his lips, then traced her lips down, her tongue exploring the crevices of his collar before flicking lightly across his nipple.

His body tensed, all his blood rushing to his cock, and he reached up to cup her ass through her khaki shorts.

She wriggled her butt, then reached back to push his hands away. "Not this time," she said.

He made some murmur of protest, his hands moving back up to stroke her thighs.

She sat up, her full weight on his stomach. "Do we have a problem, Detective?" she asked, the gleam in her eye counteracting the stern tone of her voice.

"I'm not sure," he said. "Maybe I'm not understanding tonight's lesson plan."

"Trust me," she said. Then she licked her lips, and he could almost see the lightbulb flashing over her head. She swung her leg over him and climbed off the bed, aiming a warning finger his way. "Don't move," she said.

She disappeared into the living room, then came back with the handcuffs he'd dropped on her desk. His heart picked up tempo.

"What exactly do you have in mind?" he asked.

"I guess you'll have to wait and see," she said. She crawled back into bed, raising his arms above his head. One by one she clicked the cuffs around his wrists, and when he gave a tug, he realized that she'd threaded the cuffs behind the decorative iron bars of her headboard.

"You realize that absconding with an officer's equipment is a misdemeanor," he said, managing to keep his voice light despite the heat she'd generated in his veins.

"I'll take my chances."

She straddled him again. "Fast or slow?" she asked.

"Babe, I'm so hard right now, slow would probably kill me."

Her delighted laugh teased him, and she traced her fingertips down his chest, then over his stomach. Her touch was light, teasing. At least until she reached the button for his jeans.

She was looking down, her hair falling over her face, but now she glanced up at him. Her look was smoldering, and he took a deep breath, his body shaking with need. She didn't say a word, just undid the button with ease, then started to inch down the zipper.

He held his breath as she released him, inching his jeans and boxers down until his cock jutted out. She lowered her head, then traced the tip of her tongue from his balls to the tip. Jack groaned, fighting the urge to come. He was close, so close, and he tugged against the cuffs, wanting to grab her by the hips and impale her on him, lifting her up and down until he exploded into her sweet folds.

She licked him again, less timidly, and he rocked upward.

"God, Ronnie, you're killing me." He had to force the words out.

"Killing you?" she repeated, her voice innocent. "I don't know." She closed her hand around his shaft and stroked him with a slow, fluid motion. "Looks to me like you're enjoying it immensely."

Damn the woman, he couldn't argue with that. And when she cupped his balls in one hand and closed her mouth over him, sucking him deep into the heat of her mouth, he knew he was a lost man.

She drew him in and out, setting an erotic rhythm that had his body humming. The pressure built and built, and he tugged against the headboard, trying to counteract it, wanting the sensation to last just a little longer. Deeper and deeper she drew him in, making small noises of pleasure in her throat.

It was her little sounds that finally did him in, and with a primitive groan, he succumbed, the force of his orgasm seeming to spread through his entire body, culminating in one massive, delicious release.

Exhausted, he crashed back against her pillow, his eyes barely open. Ronnie inched forward, a self-satisfied smile on her face. She curled up next to him, still fully clothed, and her fingers traced idly over his chest.

"Wow," he said.

"No kidding." She breathed in and then exhaled dramatically. "I think I may just leave you here, my permanent sex slave." She propped herself up on an elbow. "What do you think?"

"I'm all for it," he said. At the moment, he wasn't even joking. "Doesn't seem quite fair to you, though."

"No?" A devious grin spread across her face. "You'll notice that I haven't taken off the cuffs." She took his nipple between her fingers, rolling it slightly, then leaned close to whisper in his ear. "I'm hot and I'm wet and I'm not quite through with you."

As if connected to him by some magic thread, her words and her promise shot straight to his cock, making him hard all over again.

"Sweetheart," he said. "That's the best news I've heard all day."

chapter
twelve

All tied up.

Ronnie shivered, imagining all the possibilities.

Her body was on fire, and part of her wanted to simply mount him and ride him until she found release. The still-sane part of her wanted to draw it out. To make the pleasure last as long as possible. To go just a little mad from the passion.

She straddled him, her back to his face then leaned over and licked the very tip of his cock.

"Ronnie, you're killing me." His voice was raw, sensual.

She stroked him some more, teasing him with her tongue the way she wanted him to tease her. She inched down, her sex throbbing with desire. "Kiss me," she whispered, spreading her legs and arching down so his tongue could stroke her sensitive folds.

"Oh, babe," he said with a groan. He raised his head, his tongue laving her. A tremor racked her body and she writhed against him, even as she took the full length of him in her mouth.

He licked her, sucking and teasing her with his intimate kisses. His tongue delved and explored, and she was on the very edge, her body tingly with pent-up passion.

That did it. She couldn't wait anymore. She had to have him inside her.

Swinging her legs around, she turned to face him. She was on her knees, her sex ready and open for him. He was rock hard, and she made quick work of the condom, tearing open the package and sheathing him. Her eyes never left his as she clung to his waist, then lowered herself, slowly and sensually, taking him in until she could feel him deep inside of her.

They rocked together, their bodies finding the rhythm, the pressure building and building until the dam burst and Ronnie cried out, her body still trembling from the orgasm when Jack exploded inside her.

When the last tremors faded, she leaned forward, lying on top of him and breathing deeply. He smelled of sweat and sex, and her body tightened. She rolled off of him, half smiling to herself. Never before had she been this insatiable. The man did things to her, and she wasn't about to complain.

She propped herself up on one elbow, her eyes meeting his. He looked sated, and a rush of feminine power trilled up her spine. She'd put that look there. And if she had any say-so in the matter, it was a look she wanted to see again and again.

"I guess we got some blood flowing," she said. "You must be primed for working now."

He laughed. "Woman, you exhausted me. The only thing I'm good for right now is sleeping." He jangled the cuffs against the headboard. "And holding you, if you're so inclined."

"Oh, I'm inclined." She leaned over him, reaching to the floor for the jeans he'd tossed there. She rummaged until she found his key chain and the little silver key. As soon as she unbound his wrists, he rolled over, grasping her hands and holding them together.

"Next time," he said, dangling the cuffs in front of her eyes. "Next time, it's your turn."

Ronnie's breath hitched and she nodded, silently hoping that next time would be soon. Very soon.

The morning sun beat in through the apartment's window, its persistent heat waking Jack. He blinked, annoyed by the intrusion. Hell, right then, everything seemed to be an intrusion. All he wanted was to hold Ronnie close. If someone could arrange for them to stay in that bed for the rest of their lives, Jack would happily sign on the dotted line.

He had to laugh at the irony. Only days ago he'd stubbornly told Donovan that he wasn't interested in another relationship. Now, not only did he have a woman in his life, but he was terrified of losing her.

And it wasn't just the typical relationship jitters he was suffering from. He couldn't help but worry that if she didn't stay safe, he'd lose her at the hands of a murderer.

He hoped his fears were exaggerated, unfounded even. But he wasn't about to take a chance. And that's why— as much as he wanted to laze in bed reading the paper and drinking coffee—Jack had to get up. He had to go to work.

He had to go find a killer.

Quietly, so as not to wake her, he started to slide out of bed. No luck. Her fingers closed over his arm.

"Leaving so soon?"

"I need to go catch bad guys."

He heard her low sigh behind him. "I know," she said. "But it's not even seven yet. Stay with me one more minute?"

He chuckled, sliding back across the mattress toward her. "How can I turn down such a plaintive invitation?"

She snuggled close as he lay back, idly running his fingers through her hair. "What's that?" he asked, referring to a brown stain on the ceiling near the bathroom wall.

She followed his gaze. "Oh, Nat's got a leak under his sink. I've had a plumber in twice, and I think the leak's fixed, but the roof looks like hell. Not to mention Nat's floor."

"Hardwood?"

She nodded. "Just like mine."

He sat up, pulling her up with him. "Come on."

She raised an eyebrow. "Come where?"

"I'll take a look. Maybe I can fix his floor and your ceiling." He tilted his head. "You're Nat's landlord, right? You can get us in?"

She stared at him as if he was nuts. "Uh, yeah. But I thought you were gung-ho to get to work."

Jack shrugged. That was true enough. And this was work. No matter how much he told himself that he just wanted a brief moment of domesticity, the truth was he wanted a peek in Nat's apartment. A prickle of guilt nettled his skin, but he ignored it. Ronnie would be pissed if she realized, but his concern wasn't her mood; it was keeping her safe. And if she was living under a murderous psycho, that was something Jack wanted to know.

He shrugged. "I'm just going to look right now. Unless you want to keep the stain?"

"No, no," she said, pulling on shorts and a T-shirt. "I'm not complaining. If you want to play Bob Villa, I'm not going to stop you."

He followed Ronnie back into the hall and up the interior stairs to her brother's door. Except for the furnishings, the place looked exactly like Ronnie's. But where her place was warm and welcoming, Nat's was cold and uninviting. Lots of steel and hard angles. Hardly any personal items. Two photography magazines on a small table next to a single armchair. A ceramic bowl of papier-mâché fruit. A single photograph framed on the otherwise bare walls. Jack inched closer. Ronnie, about eighteen years old, near the Boathouse in Central Park.

Even the bedroom was sterile. The bed was crisply made, like something out of a magazine, and photographic equipment was neatly stacked in the plastic crates that lined the far wall. Nothing seemed out of place, nothing seemed dangerous, and yet the entire apartment felt

off. As if it was more of a movie set than a place someone lived.

Jack shook himself. He needed to back off with the
suspicions. There were other suspects out there. Just because Nat was on the list didn't mean Jack needed to start
seeing demons hiding in the shadows.

Ronnie led him to the offending sink, and Jack took a
look at the floor. The hardwood had rotted away, but the
damage was only to three planks. He could pry them up,
check the trusses and floor joints for rot, and then fix the
Sheetrock that made up Ronnie's ceiling. All in all, maybe
two days' worth of work when he factored in painting her
ceiling and revarnishing Nat's floor.

"Hopeless?" she asked.

"Not at all," he said.

"Good. I'm going broke fixing this stupid building.
First Nat's outlets shorted out, and then my air conditioner, and now the wiring for the whole building. With
the alarm work on top of everything, I'm going to have
to sell my soul to the devil."

He aimed a suggestive grin her way. "Nah. I'll give you
a better deal than the devil would. I don't want your soul.
Just your body."

She laughed. "Yeah, but you don't do electrical work."

"I don't make you tingle?"

"I stand corrected," she said, the corner of her mouth
twitching as she held back laughter.

With a grin, she headed back toward the door. Jack followed, wishing he could spend the day with her. Go to
the movies. Buy her flowers. Take a walk through Cen-

tral Park. Anything to color their relationship with a hint of normalcy.

But it wasn't normal, and it wouldn't be while this stalker was on the loose. "I need to go," he said.

She nodded. "I know."

"I want you to stay in my apartment."

"But you know better than to ask, right?" she said.

He scowled.

She touched his cheek, then pulled Nat's door shut behind him. "I'm happy to stay with you, Jack, but I have things to do. For one, I need to go down to the store and make sure Joan got the full customer list to you. And Ethan's supposed to come to talk to me about the wiring. You've got officers watching the store, and I can't hide out forever." She met his eyes, hers both fearful and defiant. "You may never solve this case. That happens a lot. I know. I've watched *Law & Order*."

"I'll solve this one," he said.

She didn't argue, just lifted herself onto her tiptoes and kissed his cheek.

His beeper went off and he checked the readout. The number was familiar, but he couldn't place it right away. He pulled out his cell phone and dialed.

Caroline Crawley answered on the first ring.

"Detective Parker," he said. "Returning your call."

"Where the hell do you get off, Officer?" she screeched, so loud he had to hold the phone away from his ear.

Ronnie's brow furrowed, but he shrugged. He had no clue what had set Mrs. Crawley off.

"I'm sorry," he said. "I don't know what you're talking about."

"Perhaps you should read the morning paper," she said, with ice in her voice. "That reporter called me up last night. Wanted me to confirm what he'd learned from Detective Parker. Wanted to know how involved I was in some online erotica group."

Jack stomach knotted, and he clenched the phone tighter. "I haven't—"

"You *bastard*. I told you I didn't want my husband to know, and now the whole world will know. And that damn reporter called while Carson was here." She snorted, and he knew with certainty that she'd hit the bourbon early that morning. "Oh, we had a hell of a time last night at the Crawley residence."

"Caroline," he said sharply.

She sucked in air, probably surprised by his use of her first name.

"I haven't talked to a reporter. And I don't intend to talk to a reporter." He paused, the full force of the situation hitting him. Someone had tipped off the reporter. Someone pretending to be Jack.

The killer.

chapter
thirteen

Jack spent A full hour with Mrs. Crawley, reassuring her that he hadn't leaked her story and promising to find out who had. That was an easy promise to make—he *was* going to catch this bastard.

Usually Jack prided himself on keeping a certain distance from his cases, but this one was personal. And he didn't intend to rest until the scumbag was behind bars.

Unfortunately, that was easier said than done. All their leads seemed to head straight to dead ends.

Jack ran his fingers through his hair, pacing in front of the dry-erase board at the front of the third-floor briefing room.

"The reporter?" he asked.

Donovan shook his head. "Young guy. Pretty green. The kid was contrite, that's for sure. But all he could tell me was that the voice was male."

"Phone records?"

"Nada," Donovan said. He shrugged. "We got the number off the kid's caller ID. A payphone in the lobby of Trump Tower."

Jack cursed, then poured himself a cup of the sludge they called coffee. "Is there any video surveillance by the payphones?"

"Are you kidding? In Trump Tower? Hell, yes. I pulled the tapes an hour ago. A couple of Spinelli's guys are holed up reviewing."

"We can pinpoint the time of the call from our reporter's cell phone," Jack said. "We should be able to nail the bastard."

"We've got it narrowed down," Donovan said. "The phone's internal clock was off a bit, but we know it was sometime between nine and ten. I've got a call in to his cellular service, too. They're pulling their records, and then we'll likely be able to nail down a better time."

Jack nodded, then rubbed his temple. "In the meantime?"

"In the meantime, we've got fifteen people using the phone in that hourlong stretch. Seven are women, so we're ruling them out for now."

"Could be a disguise," Jack said.

Donovan nodded. "I know. But you got to start somewhere."

Jack nodded. "Right. We'll start with the eight men. What do we know about them? Any clear pictures?"

"Three," Donovan said.

"Have we printed stills?"

Donovan nodded. "I knew you'd ask that." He passed

Jack a folder, and Jack flipped through the still pictures the tech guys had created from the video footage. Three average-looking guys. Not that he'd expected demonic eyes or fangs. That was the trouble with homicide. The killers looked just like everybody else.

"Let's get these to Ronnie and Joan, and also run them by the security guard at the Tower," Jack said. "Maybe they work in one of the offices." He doubted they'd have any luck. From everything they'd seen so far, they were dealing with one smart son of a bitch. Too smart to let his face get captured for posterity on a security tape.

Donovan nodded, taking the folder back.

"What about the other five?" Jack asked.

Donovan shook his head. "We got shit. I've got some of the video tech guys working on the images, trying to get something useful." He shrugged. "They said not to hold our breath."

"So we're back to nothing," Jack said, fighting to keep the frustration out of his voice.

"Looks that way."

"What about the notes? Any luck tracing the type-writer?"

Donovan snorted. "Not a damn thing," he said. "But they're still working on it. And forensics confirmed that the same typewriter did the Crawley note and the one in Brooklyn." He shrugged. "Which I coulda told you without all the scientific hocus-pocus."

"It's something," Jack said. "But it doesn't get us any-where."

"Any trace evidence from Marina's apartment?"

"I talked to Spinelli this morning. Nothing so far except the usual. City dirt. Dust. Nothing that gives us any solid clues."

Considering the short time they'd had it, Jack didn't even bother to ask about the progress on Ronnie's e-mail list. It would be a pipe dream to hope that any results were back yet.

"I talked with Tommy Jenkins," Donovan said.

Jack's ears perked up. "And?"

"He's definitely got a crush on your girl, but I don't think he's our guy. For one, he's not very smart. For another, he's got a solid alibi. The kid was in Los Angeles when Marina was killed."

"Is he the one leaving Ronnie little love notes?" Jack asked.

"The kid denies it, but he was embarrassed as hell to admit the crush in the first place. Might be him. Might not."

Jack let out a breath of frustration.

Donovan tossed the paper clip he'd been twisting onto the desk. "We've been running around like hamsters on a goddamn treadmill," he said. "Where do you want to go from here?"

"Back to the file," Jack said. "There's got to be something we've missed. We start at square one, and we go over every word, every statement, until we figure out what we missed."

"Sounds like a plan," Donovan said. He went over to his desk and dug in.

Jack did the same, breaking only for lunch. He was just

about to dig into a double cheeseburger when the phone rang—the *National Geographic* editor returning his call. By the end of the conversation, Jack had forgotten about his hunger.

He plunked the phone back in its cradle, feeling both justified and a little bewildered. Donovan looked over, his brow furrowed. "Who was that?"

"Nat Parker's editor," Jack said. "The Galápagos shoot was canceled. Nat never left the country."

"We've already got him with Marina Stephenson," Donovan said. "Can we tie him to Caroline Crawley or our Brooklyn gal?"

Jack shook his head, pacing, his thoughts going a million miles an hour. "Not with anything we've got yet. But there must be something."

He'd gotten Nat's credit card number from the magazine; the cooperative editor had pulled his expense report. So far, though, the card wasn't showing up as being used. Nat could be anywhere in the country. They didn't have a clue as to his whereabouts. For that matter, they didn't have anything concrete nailing him to the murder.

Jack said as much, and Donovan spread his hands wide. "All I've got are long shots."

"Go for it," Jack said. "We're in the fourth quarter. We need some imaginative plays."

"An affair with Caroline Crawley."

Jack just stared at him.

"Come on," Donovan said. "It's not that off-the-wall. You heard the woman. She was having some hot and heavy something going with some online hunk. Maybe they moved out of cyberspace and into a no-tell motel."

"Possible," Jack admitted. "But hard to prove. If Nat's on that e-mail list, his name's unrecognizable."

Donovan nodded, taking that in.

"There's the husband connection, too," Jack said. "It's thin, but Nat used to be a journalist."

"And Carson Crawley's an anchorman," Donovan said, picking up the thread of the conversation.

"They could have met at some work function."

Donovan nodded. "Hard to prove," he said.

"Easier if we have Caroline Crawley's cooperation."

Donovan raised an eyebrow.

Jack shrugged. "Can't hurt to try. We got her to fess up to the list. If we're right, maybe she'll fess up to Nat, too."

Traffic was a bitch, so it took twenty minutes to get to Caroline Crawley's Park Avenue apartment. Jack flashed his badge at the security guard and hit the button in the elevator for the penthouse.

The foyer was dark, the room dimmer than usual as a result of one burned-out lightbulb. Jack and Donovan exchanged a glance. Considering the cost to live there, you'd think they'd have someone whose job entailed nothing more than making sure no bulb ever burned out.

He rang the bell, then glanced at his watch. After ten, but he got the feeling Caroline Crawley wasn't the kind to go to bed early.

No answer, and so he rang again, then leaned close

to see if he heard the sounds of anyone moving within. No movement, but he did hear the faint strains of music.

Donovan pounded on the doorway. "Mrs. Crawley," he called. "Police. We'd like to talk to you."

Still no answer. Jack tried the door. Locked. And the dread was knotting in his stomach.

To hell with it.

He pulled his gun and aimed it at the lock. If he was wrong, he'd buy them a new door.

The elevator dinged, and he and Donovan whipped around, aiming their guns in unison at the parting doors.

"Holy shit." Carson Crawley's eyes went wide. "What the fuck do you think you're doing?"

"Give me your goddamn key," Donovan said, skipping the preliminaries.

Carson obeyed, and Jack pushed him aside, telling the anchorman to wait while they checked the place out.

Donovan turned the key and pushed open the door. He and Jack entered, guns at the ready.

It was a moot precaution.

Caroline Crawley was dead on the floor, and her killer was long since gone.

Ronnie couldn't decide if she should be royally pissed at Joan or truly grateful. She ran her tongue over her lips, her eyes scrolling down the daily ledger report she'd just printed.

Cash receipts were up eighty percent. *Eighty*. That was unheard of. And all because some jerk reporter went and spilled the beans about Jack's investigation and Marina's murder. Erotica was in the spotlight, and her store was reaping the benefits.

Joan practically danced into the break room. "Can you *believe* this?" she asked. "It's been nonstop customers all day. I knew it. Sex and murder. Draws them in every time."

Ronnie drummed her fingers on the tabletop.

"Oh, come on," Joan said. "You're not really pissed off that I came in and opened the store on a Monday, are you? You needed a boost in sales, and you got one. Don't look a gift horse in the mouth."

"Joan," Ronnie said. "One of our customers is *dead*."

Joan frowned, her lips pressed together. "I know," she said. "And I'm sorry. Truly I am. But that's totally unrelated."

Ronnie raised a brow. "If it's unrelated, then how come your first thought after you read the article was to come down here and open the store?"

Joan just shrugged, and Ronnie shook her head, sighing.

After Jack left, Ronnie had taken a long, relaxing bath, watched the news on television, puttered around on her dissertation work, and then wandered downstairs. Her plan was to give Ethan a call and tell him she'd be in the store doing paperwork for a few hours, and to please come by to finish the estimate and take another shot at her air conditioner.

But when she went downstairs to meet him—surprise, surprise—the store had not only been open, it had been hopping. And though Ronnie's first instinct was to shut it down, with the steady flow of customers, she'd never quite found the right moment to turn the sign in the window from Open to Closed.

Plus, the extra money *was* nice. But it felt like blood money, and the whole situation left a bad taste in her mouth.

Joan, apparently, had a less discerning palate.

"We'll talk about it later," Ronnie finally said. She glanced at the clock. "It's five. Can we compromise and shut the doors now?"

"Sure," Joan said. "That's what I was coming in to tell you. I just sold the Anaïs Nin to this really cute lawyer. I locked up after he left."

"Thanks," Ronnie said.

"And, uh, I was wondering if you'd finish closing up," Joan added.

Ronnie crossed her arms over her chest, half irritated and half amused. "In other words, you made the decision to open the store, and I get to do all the closing grunt work?"

"Well, yeah."

"And this is because...?"

Joan shrugged, her cheeks turning to pink. "I overheard what bar the lawyer was meeting his friends at. I thought I might go, you know, hang out."

Ronnie rolled her eyes. "Go."

"You're sure?"

"No," Ronnie said. "So you better get out of here before I change my mind."

Joan did, grabbing her purse and rushing out the door before Ronnie even had time to laugh.

She shook her head and got up, then grabbed the broom from the utility closet. Ethan was still upstairs, installing some replacement part on her air conditioner, and she crossed her fingers that he'd get it working today.

By the time she'd finished sweeping and going through her closing routine, Ethan stepped into the store.

"Is it working?" she asked.

He nodded. "Like a charm. I told you I wouldn't let you down."

"Yes, you did. And thank you." She glanced around the store. "Do you need to look around anymore to finish the estimate for the wiring?"

He shook his head. "No. I can get that to you tomorrow and, if it's okay, I can start work then, too."

Ronnie nodded, relieved. She hated to admit it, but the extra business that today's paper brought in was going to come in handy. For once it was nice to close the store and feel like she'd actually made a dent in her overhead.

"You guys were busy today, huh?" he said.

She nodded. "Yeah. I was just thinking about that. It's amazing what a little offhand publicity can do. No matter how morbid." She shook her head, exhaling loudly. "The world is a wacky place."

"Oh, yes." He nodded, reminding her of one of those little dogs on car dashboards.

He stood there, and she swayed back and forth, wondering what he was waiting for. "Um, do you need a check? I thought you were going to bill me."

"Oh. Right." He headed for the door. "I guess I was just wondering if you wanted to get a drink with me. I know a great little bar down the street."

Ronnie smiled. Apparently Ethan was trying to put his assertiveness training into practice. "Oh, Ethan. That's very sweet. But I've got plans this evening."

"Right. Of course you do," he said. "It was just a passing thought."

He looked so let down, Ronnie almost changed her mind. Too bad he hadn't come down a few minutes earlier. Joan probably would have relished the chance to have a shy young man to mold.

"Well," he said. "I guess I should go now. The air works great. And I'll come by again tomorrow."

"That's great," she said. She gave him a bright smile that she hoped made up for turning down his invitation. "I'm looking forward to getting the place all fixed up."

She locked up behind Ethan, then leaned against the door with a sigh. *Air-conditioning.* What a lovely word.

And she knew the perfect way to celebrate the return of reasonable temperatures. She was going to go upstairs, get naked, lie on the bed…and wait for Jack.

chapter
fourteen

Despite a complete search of the Crawleys' apartment, the cops hadn't found any trace of the killer, or any specific evidence that Caroline Crawley knew Nat. In fact, other than Caroline's dead body, the only thing wrong in the apartment was Carson Crawley's desktop computer— smashed to bits with a heavy bronze statue. Whether or not that was the killer's attempt to cover up e mail evidence, they might never know.

In response to Jack's pointed questions, Carson said he didn't recall a Nathan Parker, but admitted that he met too many young journalists to remember them all. He did say that he suspected his wife was having an affair, but he'd never been able to find any proof. The police had no better luck.

Which meant that they were exactly where they'd started, only with one more dead body. Things were not looking up.

Donovan was working on getting a search warrant. Jack prayed a search of Nat's apartment would turn something up. They were including the bookstore in the warrant, too, and Jack knew Ronnie wasn't going to like that, no matter how much she understood that the cops were just doing their job. She'd be pissed, and Jack wanted to tell her it was coming. Give her a little fair warning. Smooth the way.

Ronnie's apartment was dark when he got there, and at first Jack wondered if she'd gone out. The possibility grated.

More and more, he was leaning toward Nat as the killer. And while Jack didn't think Nat Parker would harm his own sister, Jack sure as hell had no guarantees, and he wasn't about to play roulette with Ronnie's safety. He'd beefed up the patrol around her shop and ordered unmarked cars to sit at the front and rear entrances. It gave him a sense of security, and Ronnie didn't need to know.

He waved at the heavy-lidded officer in the black Lincoln. The guy waved back, a cup of coffee in one hand. Jack slipped inside the building and headed up the stairs, sure the officer was more than a little jealous.

Ronnie had given him her spare key, so even if she was out, he could wait for her—and then read her the riot act when she returned.

He twisted the lock, going over *exactly* what he'd say to the cops outside when he found out Ronnie had simply sauntered off down the street. He was bordering on being unreasonable, and he knew it. But, dammit, two women had been murdered. He didn't want to bring that fact to his relationship with Ronnie, but he didn't have a choice. The case—the murders—colored everything. And if she was putting herself in danger, he damn sure wanted to know about it.

Then he pushed the door open…and saw the rose petals on the floorboards.

His fear evaporated, replaced with a sense of relief so palpable he felt it spreading through his veins. She was safe.

Not only was she safe, but she seemed instinctively to know his needs. To know that he needed moments away from the horror, just as she surely did. Time for just the two of them. A little bit of normalcy. The eye of the storm.

Because when the warrant came through, he was certain there'd be a storm.

He moved toward her bedroom door. He had an inkling of what was behind there, on the bed, in the dark, and damned if he didn't want to sink down into the mattress with her and forget everything he'd learned today.

His body tightened at the thought, and he took long, deep breaths, trying to rein in the control that Ronnie had set loose.

His hand hesitated over the light switch, but he didn't turn it on. She'd planned a seduction, and he wasn't going to ruin it in a glare of lights. As her lover, he wanted to open up to her. To hold her tight and tell her about his day. To confide in her about Nat and the rest of the investigation.

As a cop, he knew that was impossible. She was his key suspect's sister. And no matter how he felt about her, he couldn't compromise the investigation by feeding her information that might make it back to Nat.

He didn't believe Ronnie had any knowledge of what Nat was up to. Hell, he didn't believe that Ronnie even knew Nat was still in town. But Spinelli wasn't as convinced. No threats, no little erotic postcards had come Ronnie's way. In Spinelli's mind, that made her a suspect, as well.

In Jack's, it just made her lucky.

Either way, it meant she was embroiled in the investigation. And that meant his lips were sealed. No matter how much it might hurt her in the end. He could tell her about the warrant, but no more. And that was allowable only because it would be signed within hours. And he was right here to make sure their suspect's sister didn't tamper with evidence.

Mentally, he cringed. He knew in his gut she wouldn't do such a thing, and he hated even thinking it. But he was a cop first.

"Jack?" Her voice, low and sultry, drifted to him from the bedroom.

"It's me," he said.

"Well, what's taking you so long?"

He couldn't help his smile, and as he headed toward the bedroom door, he reached up and loosened his tie. Out of habit, this time, not from the oppressive heat, and he realized that her air conditioner had been fixed.

That alone was reason to celebrate.

He came bearing bad news, but he pushed gamely forward, hoping that when the time came, she wouldn't feel compelled to shoot the messenger.

As he got closer to the bedroom, he heard the soft music drifting out from within. He closed his hand over the brass doorknob and pushed in, his eyes widening at the erotic feast laid out before him. At least a dozen candles dotted the room, circling the bed and lighting it in a dim, orange glow.

Two glasses of wine sat on the bedside table, a pair of handcuffs next to them. But what really made his heart skip a beat was Ronnie, completely naked and bathed in candlelight, her fingers idly stroking the inside of her thigh.

His cock hardened, and he fought the urge to forget the damn warrant and just sink inside of her.

A sultry smile spread across her face. "Ready for another lesson?"

Every nerve in his body seemed to tighten, as if tugged together like a drawstring bag. "Ronnie, we need—"

"I only need one thing," she said. "And that's you."

"Ronnie, please." His voice sounded hoarse, and it was all he could do to force the word out.

"Watch me," she said.

He started to protest once again, but she drew her hand up her thigh, spreading her legs as she did so. Her dark curls were damp, and her folds were slick, almost glistening in the candlelight. Jack swallowed, a wash of pure desire crashing down on him. He needed to talk to her, to tell her what was coming. Intellectually, he knew that. But he needed to make love to her more.

"Make love to me, Jack," she said.

He groaned, her words caressing him, and he shifted. His groin throbbed with need and he felt like a heel, but he knew what he was going to do. Whether it was right or wrong to put his needs first, he didn't know. All he knew was that he had to have her. Had to lose himself in her. Had to satisfy the persistent throbbing in his groin.

He told himself he didn't want to hurt her. Told himself it would be rude to spoil her elaborate seduction with something so crass as murder and procedure.

He told himself all that, but the truth was, he simply wanted her. Wanted this moment, a mere pinpoint in time where there was nothing between them, and he wasn't going to hurt her.

Knowing he shouldn't, but powerless to stop himself, he moved to the edge of the bed and, without a word, stripped off his pants.

Ronnie snuggled up into the curve of Jack's arm. They'd made love without words, wild and hard and fast. She'd loved it, the way he'd held her down and plunged into her, as if she'd generated a compelling need in him that he had to satisfy right then.

Smiling to herself, she snuggled closer, hooking her thigh over his, her body still seeking his heat even when she was sated. He *had* needed her. And all because she'd seduced him. A rush of feminine power shot through her and she kissed his chest.

His fingers traced up and down her back. It was comfortable, nice, and she hoped it would never end. She was in love with this man. She wasn't entirely sure when it had happened, but the end result was the same. She loved him. And she was certain he felt the same.

"Hey," she whispered, "want to go find some sustenance? And then after dinner maybe we could have a little noncaloric dessert?"

A low chuckle rumbled in his chest, and he shifted. He propped a pillow up against her wrought-iron headboard and sat up, pulling her up beside him. "That's appealing," he said, then kissed her lightly on the top of her head.

"Good." She started to scoot to the edge of the bed, intending to go see what, if anything, she had in her refrigerator. He pulled her back.

"We need to talk," he said.

She stilled, something in his voice sending chills up her spine. She twisted, turning to face him. "What?" she said.

He took a deep breath, and she saw a hint of fear in his eyes. It scared her, and she took his hands. "Jack? What?"

"I want you to know that I love you, Ronnie. I don't know when it happened, exactly, but I do." He stroked her cheek. "You'll remember that?"

"Oh, Jack." She laughed, realizing the fear she'd seen had been due to cold feet. Tears pooled in her eyes at the same time a goofy grin spread over her face. "Thank you," she said. "For saying it first." She kissed him, the kiss somehow different because now he really belonged to her. "I love you, too."

He cupped her cheek in his hand. "Ronnie—"

His pager beeped, the harsh sound all the more irritating because of the moment it was interrupting. He grabbed it from the bedside table and glanced at the read-out. His face hardened and he closed his eyes. Ronnie counted ten beats, then started to worry.

"Jack?"

He opened his eyes, staring deep into hers. "We've got a warrant, Ronnie. We're going to search the building."

He might as well have slapped her.

Ronnie's whole body recoiled from his words, and she grabbed the sheet, pulling it tight around her chest, instinctively seeking some barrier between them. "What?" she asked.

"You heard me," he said.

"I heard you say you loved me, too," she said, a confused wash of anger and betrayal twisting in her veins. "I'm beginning not to trust my ears."

He flinched but didn't look away. "Ronnie, please—"

"Please? Oh, no. *Please* isn't part of the equation. A warrant?" She stood up, propelled by the force of her anger. "You think *I'm* involved? You want to search my building? Dammit, Jack. Just ask me. I'd consent." She lifted her chin. "Or I would have five minutes ago. Now I'm not so sure."

"The warrant doesn't include your apartment," he said. His voice was all business, and that irritated her even more. "Just the store, the storage area and Nat's apartment."

Nat.

Suddenly, she realized. They thought her brother was

a killer. "That's absurd," she said, with a strangled little laugh. "Nat?"

Jack wasn't laughing, and a hard rock formed in the pit of Ronnie's stomach. She wasn't sure if it was anger or fear. She got off the bed, then pulled her robe on and tied it tight around her waist.

"Ronnie," he said, stepping into his slacks. "I'm just doing my job. Looking at the facts."

"What facts?" she snapped, pacing the room. "He's not even here. He's in the Galápagos, remember? So how could he have killed Marina?"

"He's not," Jack said. "The shoot was canceled. He didn't get on a plane."

His words were gentle, almost apologetic, but even so they hit her with a force so brutal she almost stumbled. As it was, she had to pull the chair out from her vanity and sit down.

Jack moved toward her, and she tensed. She didn't want his comfort right then. She was angry and confused, and she didn't want any touch other than her own arms hugging herself tightly.

Jack regarded her for a moment, then turned away, moving instead to flick on the overhead light. One by one he blew out the candles. The fantasy was over. Brutal reality had returned.

There was only the one chair in the room, so he leaned against the wall, facing her. "Did you hear me?" he asked.

"I heard you," she whispered. "I don't believe you."

"It's true. Whether you want to believe it or not, it's true."

She hugged herself. "Then there's an explanation. Something simple. Something funny. I know Nat. He couldn't do those things."

"No one ever really knows anyone else," Jack said. "I've been a cop long enough to realize that."

She blinked. "So I guess I don't really know you." She was feeling angry, and more than ready to pick a fight.

Jack, apparently, wasn't having any of it. "I know this hurts, Ronnie. But I have to ask you a question. I have to know. Do you know where your brother is?"

She blinked, her eyes brimming with tears. "Why are you doing this? Why now?"

"You told me you understood. That I couldn't just turn the cop part on and off."

"He's my *brother*. Even if you don't know him, you know me. And *I* know he couldn't have done the horrible things you're suggesting."

He reached for her and she jerked away, moving to the far side of the room, the bed providing a barrier between them.

She wanted him to come to her. To fight past the pain. To hold her close and rock her and tell her it was going to be okay.

He didn't.

"I need you to answer the question, Ronnie," Jack said. "Please don't make this harder than it is."

"You knew," she said. "When you came over tonight, you knew they were getting the warrant. And yet you still…"

He closed his eyes, a muscle twitching in his cheek. "I'm sorry," he said.

"Well, that's really not enough."

"I know." A beat. Then another. "Answer the question, Ronnie. Where is he?"

"I don't know," she said. Her shoulders sagged. "I wish I did. Believe me, Detective. I wish I did."

"I've got patrol cars watching the building. Watching for him, and watching out for you."

She shivered, the implications unnerving. "He wouldn't do anything to hurt me," she whispered.

"Two women are dead, Ronnie."

She blinked. "Two?"

"Caroline Crawley," he said. "A gunshot wound to the neck." He looked at her, his eyes intense. "Does Nat own a gun?"

"No." She shook her head, realizing she really didn't know. "I don't know. I don't think so." She hugged herself, trying to get her bearings.

"Did Nat know her? From his days in journalism? Maybe socialize with her?"

"I don't know." She shook her head. This was all too much. "What happened to innocent until proven guilty?"

"That's my job," Jack said. "To prove him guilty."

"*If* he is."

Jack didn't answer, and Ronnie didn't say anything else. Nat wasn't their killer, but no matter how many times she said so, Jack wasn't going to listen.

Despite her certainty, doubt edged into her mind. She pushed it away, hating him for making her think—even for an instant—that Nat could do such a thing. She knew her brother. It simply wasn't possible.

She blinked, a single tear spilling down her cheek. Maybe she was being unreasonable, close-minded. But she couldn't help it. Between her lover and her brother, how else could she choose? And she resented having to choose at all.

"Get out," she said.

"Ronnie…" He took a tentative step toward her.

She took one backward, away from him.

"Ronnie? Are you going to be okay?"

She laughed, a coarse, hard sound. "Just go."

"As soon as Donovan gets here with the warrant, I'll need you to let us in Nat's apartment," he said. "And into the store."

She gaped at him, wondering when she'd fallen through the rabbit hole. Then she nodded. "Send Donovan up, then," she said, hoping she was making herself clear. Jack wasn't welcome.

"Go," she said. She pulled her robe tighter around her. He moved to the door, then hesitated. She turned away.

And she didn't turn back until she heard the door click closed behind him.

chapter
fifteen

Ronnie let them in, and then went back to her apartment, staying there during the search. In a way, Jack was
relieved. He'd hurt her. He knew that. But he couldn't
focus on that now, and having her around would only
distract him.

The team spread out, starting at the top and working
their way down.

They found little in Nat's apartment. They confiscated
the books of negatives and the reels of undeveloped film.
No photographs had turned up in the case, but it was possible he took pictures of his victims. Most stalkers liked
to keep a souvenir, and Jack doubted Nat would stray far
from the profile.

In the bathroom, his eyes drifted to the rotten wood
under the sink. His stomach twisted. Hell of a thing to
get melancholy over, but he suddenly regretted not hav-

ing yet fixed Ronnie's ceiling. He hoped to hell he'd still get the chance.

After several hours, they finished in Nat's apartment. No smoking gun, but the team had collected all the appropriate fiber samples. The lab would try to match them to fibers found at the scene of the Crawley and Stephenson murders. They'd know in a few days if there was a match. If there was, it was one more nail in Nat Parker's coffin. Either way, they'd keep on plugging, trying to compile the evidence. Build the case.

And they still had to find Nat.

Jack followed the team down to the storage level, his mind sorting through the possibilities. He believed that Ronnie didn't know where her brother was. She'd been genuinely surprised when he'd told her Nat hadn't left the country. Even more, he trusted her. She might be furious at him, but he didn't believe she'd deliberately mislead him.

Their killer was close, though. Probably read the papers, and that's what triggered Caroline Crawley's murder.

"Parker," Donovan yelled, interrupting his thoughts. "Get a load of this."

Jack followed his partner's voice, finding him buried among some boxes. Someone had arranged them into a cubicle space, and a manual typewriter was perched on the floor, half-hidden by an old tarp. The logo was barely visible—Royal.

Jack met Donovan's eyes. If his hunch was correct, that typewriter had a slightly raised *e*.

* * *

It was noon the next day before Ronnie remembered to eat. She'd sleepwalked through the previous evening, her only jolt coming when they'd sealed off her storage area with crime tape and carted her dad's ancient typewriter away.

She kept telling herself this was a nightmare, and she'd wake up from it. But she knew that wasn't true, and she couldn't hide out in her pajamas forever. Feeling sluggish, as if she were recovering from the flu, she stumbled to the kitchen and brewed some Earl Grey tea.

The real hell of it was that Jack had actually made her start doubting herself. She'd never done that before— *never.*

She believed in Nat. He'd practically raised her. He'd taught her how to ride a two-wheeler. He'd taken her to her first R-rated movie. He'd given her first boyfriend the third degree.

He was her brother, not a killer. He was the man who'd held her hand through her hideous divorce, and who'd never hesitated when she'd needed a shoulder to cry on. He had his faults—she wasn't blind. He drifted, lacked focus. But so did a lot of people. This time, apparently, his drifting had gotten him in trouble. He'd probably been fired from the shoot, and then decided to take off on one of his photography sprees, shooting the Appalachians or something.

She gnawed on her lip. The only thing was, in the past, he'd always told her before he left. This time, nothing.

She shook off the doubt, then took her tea to the table

and pulled out a notepad and a pen. Jack was focusing on Nat; she'd focus on the other possibilities.

She drew a line down the page, numbered it and started writing down the name or description of every customer who'd gone to one of her lectures more than once. Then she added Ethan and Joan, even though Jack said they'd both checked out. Tommy was on the list, too, even though he seemed sweet and generally harmless. Jack had said he'd been in California, but didn't people in the movies always manage to fake an alibi?

An hour later, she had a thin list and no concrete idea what to do with it. No one jumped out as a killer. She'd had no brilliant burst of inspiration. No flash of insight that would save her brother.

Frustrated, she pushed back from the table. She pulled her hair back, catching it in a rubber band left lying on the counter from the newspaper. She headed toward the fire escape, needing a little fresh air.

The window was large, and she easily climbed onto the grating. The fire escape ran from the living-room window to the bedroom window, providing escape from both. A ladder hung down on the right, connecting her apartment to Nat's.

She leaned against the railing for a while, breathing in the thick afternoon air. It was hot and sultry outdoors, in stark contrast to her now frosty apartment. But the heat felt good, as if she needed thawing. After a while, though, she got tired and turned to go back inside. That's when she saw it.

A small pink envelope on the grating, right under her window.

She must have stepped right over it without even noticing. An icy chill chased down her spine, and she turned, this way and that, looking for the messenger.

Nobody. She was all alone.

Her heart pounded in her chest as she eyed the envelope, staring at it as if it was a wild dog she had to stare down. It looked crisp, not at all limp or faded from the heat, and she wondered how long it had been out there.

Her instinct was to pick it up, but she fought the urge. It might be nothing, of course, but she didn't really believe that.

The stalker had found her. A dubious honor. One she could certainly live without.

More calmly than she would have thought herself capable, she climbed back into the apartment, careful not to touch the note. Her throat was tight, her entire body on alert, poised for flight.

She went straight for the phone and dialed.

He answered on the first ring.

"Jack," she said, her voice unfamiliar to her ears. "I need you."

Jack arrived with a team, and now cops bustled around, dusting for fingerprints all over the fire escape. Ronnie sat on her sofa, curled up under a quilt that Jack had gently tucked around her body.

She had the shakes, and that bothered her. She didn't

like being afraid. And right then she was afraid. Very afraid. For her safety, and for her brother.

According to Jack, the note was odd compared to the others. Softer. Almost romantic. And all the scarier for it. It was from the Song of Songs. Biblical. *My beloved is mine, and I am his… By night on my bed I sought him whom my soul loveth.*

Ronnie had once found the words beautiful. Now she found them terrifying.

She watched Jack work, finding some comfort in his efficient movements. She'd been furious at him last night, but the fury had faded, replaced by fear and a twinge of hurt. Intellectually, she knew he couldn't tell her about the investigation. Emotionally, though, he'd ripped her to shreds.

But she loved him. No matter what, she did. When she'd seen the note, her first thought was of Jack. Not the detective, but the man. She wanted to feel his arms around her, wanted him to hold her and make it better. She wanted him forever, and she hoped she hadn't screwed up by pushing him away.

When the officers finished, they left, leaving her alone with Jack. He sat on the edge of the coffee table. "We need to talk," he said.

She nodded, but couldn't quite form words.

"The typewriter matched," he said, his words making her cold despite the warmth of the quilt. "We got the preliminary results back early this morning." He took her hand. "I'm sorry, babe. I can't tell you how sorry I am."

She closed her eyes, letting the weight of the truth

settle around her, letting the noose tug just a bit tighter around Nat's throat.

He took a deep breath. "There was more evidence, too. It's not good."

She licked her lips, looking at him, afraid to ask.

"The negatives and film canisters. We developed some of the film. Pictures of Marina and of Caroline. Like I said, it doesn't look good. We've already got an arrest warrant. Now we just have to find him."

Her eyes burned with tears, and she hugged herself. She was living a nightmare, and the only way through it was to take one step at a time. "Even if you're right, even if it is Nat, why would he send this to me?" The words were intimate, and bile rose in her throat as she imagined her brother whispering those words to her. *No.*

"I don't know," Jack said. "I have a theory. You won't like it."

She pressed her lips together, steeling herself. "What?"

"He wants you. He cherishes you. But he can't have you. And so he's been projecting on other women."

"But murder?" she said, trying hard to keep emotion out of it and look only at the facts.

"Marina's murder was an accident," he said. "We're almost positive. Caroline's was probably to cover up evidence. Hide a connection."

"But why the note to me now? Why not before?"

Jack's face hardened. "I think you *have* gotten notes before. The roses, the chocolate. He was romancing you."

"He's my brother," she whispered, her stomach roiling. "You have to be wrong."

"Half brother. That might make all the difference in his twisted mind."

She shook her head, wanting to keep his words at bay. "No." She wanted to scream the word. She took a deep breath. "And even if he left the roses, the chocolate, then why this? Why now?"

"He knows we're on to him. And he knows you have someone else." He met her eyes. "Or you did."

She squeezed his hand. "Do."

Relief flashed in his eyes, and he continued. "I think he's cracking. The facade is chipping away. His fantasy is being knocked down, and it's making him dangerous."

She closed her eyes, a futile attempt to block out the horror. "You're wrong," she said. "You have to be."

"I hope so." He stroked her hair. "Oh, sweetheart, I hope so."

She pressed her lips together, undone by how strongly she wanted him. Not sex. Not physical contact. But *him*. "Jack," she said, her voice a plea. "I'm sorry."

He pressed a finger over her lips, shaking his head slightly. "Don't. You don't have anything to be sorry about."

"I believe in my brother," she said, taking his hand in both of hers. "There has to be an explanation. Something you've missed. Some reason that he looks guilty. Smoke and mirrors." She released a shaky breath. "But I don't know what. I honestly don't know." She swallowed, meeting his eyes. "But I do know one thing for certain. I love you." A tear spilled down her face, and she wiped it away. "We can get past this, right?"

He raised their joined hands, kissing the soft part at the base of her thumb. "I love you, too, sweetheart. That will see us through."

He pulled her close then, into an embrace. His fingers stroked her back. She wanted to lose herself in his touch, to forget about what he'd told her even if only for a few minutes.

"I know what you need," Jack said.

"Yes," she murmured, her voice breathy.

He sat back, away from her, and she blinked in confusion. He reached down and pulled up his pant leg, revealing an ankle holster. "I want you to keep it with you."

She blanched, sitting back and raising an eyebrow. "A gun? That wasn't exactly what I had in mind."

"I can't be with you all the time, and I want you safe. I've got cars watching the building, but they were watching last night and no one saw our Casanova leave that note."

She nodded. He was right. "I've never shot a gun," she said.

"Nothing to it." He demonstrated what to do, telling her it was a semiautomatic with thirteen rounds in the magazine. "There's one in the chamber, so you're ready to go. Aim and fire, and don't stop firing until the gun's empty. This isn't target practice. It doesn't have to be neat, it just has to keep you alive."

Ronnie nodded. If Jack was right—if Nat was the killer—she didn't know if she could shoot him. But she kept that to herself. It didn't matter. Nat couldn't have done those things, and soon enough Jack would find the real murderer.

She tested the weight of the gun in her hand. It felt heavy, foreign. And inherently dangerous. "I don't like guns," she said.

"You'll like them even less if one shoots you."

She nodded. "You're right. I know you're right." She exhaled loudly, then set the gun on the table. "Thank you," she said. "I hope I won't need it."

"So do I," he said.

She tugged at his tie. "I know what I *do* need," she said.

And this time, thank goodness, he understood perfectly.

He hadn't lost her. She was still his. Thank God, she was still his.

Over and over, Jack repeated the words to himself, like a mantra as he thrust in and out, watching her face. He didn't want to stop looking at her, and never once while they made love had he closed his eyes.

He'd been terrified that she wouldn't understand, wouldn't forgive him for pursuing her brother. But she had. She loved him. And, so help him, he loved her more than he'd ever thought possible.

They'd started out slow, sweet. But she'd urged him on, grinding against him, begging for more, as if she needed an intensity in their lovemaking to counteract the intensity of her life.

He'd met her demands, and now he pumped inside her hot, wet heat, a slick sheen of sweat coating his body. She was beneath him, her legs spread wide, her mouth parted and her eyes closed. She was beautiful, and she belonged to him.

She made little noises of pleasure, and with each little sound, he thrust harder, bringing himself closer to the brink.

Little tremors took her body, and he knew she was close. He slipped his hand between them, teasing her clit as he thrust down. She moaned, arching her back and raising her hips up to meet him.

"Jack," she whispered. "Oh, Jack. Yes. Yes, please. I'm so close."

The sound of his name on her lips turned him on even more, and he came, his body trembling against hers with a force that took her over the edge, as well. She cried out, her muscles contracting around him, squeezing him dry, until he collapsed on her, exhausted and satisfied.

They stayed like that for a long time. And then she rolled over and kissed him softly on the lips.

"I love you," she said.

He kissed the tip of her nose. "I love you, too."

They drifted off, the sound of Jack's cell phone startling them back to reality along with the first strains of the morning light. She looked at him, her eyes like a deer's caught in headlights. Jack checked the caller ID, then picked up. "Parker."

"We found him," Donovan said. "Credit card came through. A cheap motel in Brooklyn. He's there now. Spinelli's heading over."

Jack ended the conversation and clicked off, shifting in the bed to face Ronnie. "It's time," he said. "We're going to go arrest your brother."

chapter
sixteen

Ronnie wanted to go to the station to see Nat, but Jack told her to wait. There were procedural things to be taken care of, and she'd end up stuck in a hall for hours.

Instead, she stayed in her apartment, pacing the floor. The only break she took from pacing was to call Paul, the store's lawyer, and ask him to find a good criminal attorney. He promised to do what he could, and Ronnie went back to pacing.

After about an hour of that, she decided to go to the store until Jack called, hoping that work would keep her mind off her brother. Joan was already there when she got downstairs, working on the catalog. Ethan was in the break room, doing what work he could without having access to the sealed-off third floor where most of the electrical panels and stuff were located.

Joan was humming a little ditty, bobbing her head in time with her own off-key ramblings.

"I take it you had a good time last night," Ronnie said.

"Oh, yeah. I knew that lawyer was worth chasing after."

"What kind of law?" Ronnie asked. "Civil or criminal?"

"Medical malpractice," Joan said. "Boob jobs gone bad."

"A pity," Ronnie said, forcing a light tone. "Nat might be in the market for a criminal attorney." She filled Joan in, the act of telling someone cathartic somehow.

"Nat," Joan said, shaking her head. "I don't believe it."

"I know," Ronnie said. "I don't, either. But there's all this evidence piled up against him. It's perplexing." She nibbled on her lower lip. "I hope Paul calls back soon. Nat needs a decent lawyer."

"You're going to go down to the precinct and see him, right?"

Ronnie nodded. "When Jack calls me."

Joan cocked her head. "That might take forever."

She glanced at her watch. "I'll give him two hours, then I'll page him and see what's going on."

They managed to get some work done on the catalog, although the conversation felt forced. They danced around the actual language of the erotic volumes they wanted to include. As if saying the wrong thing would make the whole house of cards just collapse on top of them.

"You're sure you're okay?" Joan repeatedly asked.

After the fourth inquiry, Ronnie aimed her pencil at her friend. "Ask me that once more, and I swear I'm going to smack you."

Joan laughed, but Ronnie was half-serious. She was on edge and wasn't about to be held responsible for flying off the handle at anyone.

When the mail came at two, Ronnie was ready for the break.

"Bill, bill, bill, magazine, bill." Joan sorted through the mail. She paused, holding up a large flat envelope. "A catalog, maybe? It's addressed to you, not the store."

Ronnie took it, curious. She slid her finger under the flap, loosening the glue, then peered inside.

A single photograph.

A feeling of dread built in her stomach, and even though she had nothing tangible to base it on, she knew this would be bad. With her lips pressed together, she pulled the eight-by-ten glossy out.

Her and Jack. Naked. The very first time they'd made love.

Her heart floated up into her throat, and she struggled not to vomit. Whoever had taken the shot had been right there—*right there*. Just inches away on her fire escape. Close enough to touch.

Close enough to see everything.

Watching her and Jack. Watching them make love.

Ronnie shivered, wondering what else he'd watched, and for how long.

Jack met her where she sat outside an interview room. "Are you ready?"

Ronnie nodded, wanting to see her brother, but at the same time dreading it.

Jack squinted down at her. "Ronnie?"

"I'm sorry." She took a breath, meeting his eyes. "Something happened."

Jack's posture shifted, almost imperceptively, but she noticed the tension. "What?"

Wordlessly, she handed him the envelope. He opened it, glanced at the photo, then slipped it back into the envelope. His face remained entirely passive, a tightening in his jaw the only hint of the rage she knew was right there under the surface.

Ronnie didn't have quite that much self-control, and the second Jack met her eyes again, the dam burst. Tears spilled from her eyes, and her shoulders shook.

Jack was at her side immediately, pulling her to her feet and holding her close in his arms. She clung to him, her anchor in a sea of despair, until the tears stopped.

"You okay?" he asked, concern lining his face.

"As much as possible," she said. She wiped her eyes, then glanced toward the door. "I'm going to go talk to him."

With some hesitation, she took the envelope back. She didn't know if she'd ask Nat about the picture, but she wanted to have it with her just in case.

Steeling herself, she marched through the door.

Her brother glanced up. Dark bags hung under his eyes, and his hair was a mess. He needed a shave, and his eyes were bloodshot.

"I'm innocent," he said. "You of all people should believe in me."

She aimed a smile at him, but she was afraid it wavered. "I believe you, Nat. I really do. But I don't understand how the police have all this evidence."

"It's all bullshit," he said. "I need a lawyer, McDonald. The public defender they got for me's an idiot."

"I'm already looking for someone," she promised. Her eyes burned, and she blinked back tears. "But Nat," she whispered, "I need to know what's going on. You lied to me about the trip. You told me you were out of the country. Think about how that looks. To me. To the police."

His shoulders sagged a little, and he ran his fingers through his hair, making it stand on end. "I know," he said. "Don't you think I know that?"

"Then what's the real story?" she asked.

"I was embarrassed." He rolled one shoulder, then looked her in the eye. "You were so proud of me, and then they canceled the shoot. And I was just embarrassed. It's a stupid excuse, I know. But it's the truth."

"So you're living somplace else?"

"Motel," he said. "Cheap." He met her gaze, his eyes plaintive. "I didn't want you to think I'd failed."

Her heart twisted. "Nat, I'd never think that. The shoot fell through. Big deal. It's not your fault."

He shrugged but said nothing more.

She took a deep breath, then pressed on. "But what about the pictures of those two women? What about the typewriter?" She almost mentioned the photograph in her hand, but didn't. She sat the envelope on the table. His eyes drifted to it, but he didn't ask.

"I was seeing Marina," he admitted. "We met at one of your lectures." He blushed a little, reminding her of a little boy. "And Caroline and I…" He trailed off. "It's embarrassing."

"Nat, you've been indicted for *murder.*"

"We had an affair," he spit out. "But I'd never, ever harm either of them. I wouldn't. I mean, if I'd killed them, would I have kept the pictures in my apartment?"

"What about the typewriter?" she asked.

"It wasn't me. Anybody can get up there. Half the time you keep the third floor unlocked during working hours. A customer could get up there. Anyone." Desperation laced his voice, and she saw the fear in his eyes. "You have to believe me, Ron. You have to believe I didn't do those things."

She was silent for a moment, and his gaze dropped to the envelope, but still he didn't ask. After a moment, she nodded. "It'll be okay, Nat." She squeezed his hand. "Really."

He grabbed her hand. "Ron, I love you. I'm scared."

She tried to give him a reassuring smile but wasn't sure she succeeded. The horror of what he was accused of pressed down around her. Her throat closed up and she struggled to take a breath. She wanted to cry, but for his sake managed to fight back the tears.

"I know," she said, forcing the words out. "I'll do everything I can. I…I have to go." She tugged her hand free and managed to get out of the room before the dam burst.

In the hall, she leaned back against the closed door, her body sagging with the strain of putting on a happy front. Jack stood in front of her. "He had an explanation for everything," she said, the tears breaking free.

"I know. I'm sorry, sweetheart, but I just don't believe what he's telling us."

She nodded, breathing deep to stave off the flood of tears. "I know," she said, catching her breath. She met Jack's eyes. "I don't know what to believe anymore. All I know is I'm scared."

The next day, the pain Ronnie felt at Nat's arrest was just as fresh. He was scheduled to be arraigned soon, and Jack was still convinced he was guilty.

The entire situation had freaked Ronnie out. She believed in her brother—she *did*. But Jack's certainty and the evidence weighed on her. And she felt guilty even toying with the idea that he might really have done those horrible things.

The idea that her brother was a stalker and a murderer was bad enough. But the picture of her and Jack…that made her physically ill.

The previous night, Jack had installed a window shade behind her curtains. Never again was anyone looking in her windows.

Joan stepped around one of the bookshelves. "Are you okay?" she asked.

Ronnie nodded. "I'm fine," she said. "I'll be better once we get past the arraignment." She cocked her head. "You have the other key now, right?"

Nat's possessions had been taken and logged, including his keys. Jack had retrieved one for her—the master key that opened the front door and led from the interior stairs into the store. She had a feeling she'd be spending a lot of time in court and away from the store, and she wanted Joan to have full access to the upper floors.

"Yup," Joan said, rattling her key ring. "It's so icky to think he lived right above you. That he could come into the store anytime he wanted. I mean, do you think he came down here and read the erotica and—"

"Joan," Ronnie said sharply, holding up a hand. "He's my brother, and I'm not convinced he's guilty. So I'd *really* rather not think about that."

"Right," Joan said. "Of course." She glanced around the store, fidgeting a little. "I guess I'll head on out. You're sure you're okay closing up?"

"Fine," Ronnie said, forcing her thoughts back to work. "I'll see you tomorrow."

The bell jangled as Joan left, and Ronnie finished dusting the shelves. Ethan was still working in the break room, and she headed that direction to see how he was coming along.

"It'll go faster when I can get back on the third floor," he said. He sounded peevish, unlike his usual self.

"They said they'd unseal it soon," she assured him. She eyed his work. It seemed to be taking forever, especially considering how few wires and things were pulled out from the walls. "Um, how long is all this going to take?"

His toolbox was on the table between them, a copy of *Getting to Yes* peeking out from among the wrenches and screwdrivers. He pulled out a length of wire, holding it taut between his hands. Ronnie took a step backward, then laughed at herself. She really was on edge.

"Just a few more days," he said. "So long as I can get to the third floor." He looked down in the direction of his shoes. "I'll miss coming here. I'll miss you."

She tried to smile. "That's sweet, Ethan. I'll miss you, too. Maybe I'll have a short or something for you to fix," she added, and then laughed awkwardly at her own stupid joke.

He didn't laugh. Just twisted the wire in his hands. He briefly met her gaze then looked away as he said, "Well, would you go out for a drink with me or something?"

"Oh, Ethan, I'd love to. But I'm seeing someone and, well, I really can't."

For a second she imagined that his soft features hardened, but when she looked again, it was the same old Ethan. The light, she assumed, and her imagination.

He nodded. "Right. Sure." He shook his head. "Same story all the time. I should be used to it now, right?"

He twisted the wire in his hands some more, and she swallowed, noticing for the first time how big he was despite his boyish looks. He moved around the side of the table, almost casually, but with definite purpose.

"I mean, I'm just trying to be assertive, you know," he said. The lines in his face became more rigid, defined, as if he was fighting anger.

A spring of fear bubbled up in Ronnie's gut, and she tensed, calculating the best route past him and to the door.

"I'm just trying to go after what I want like all those books say you should do. But what I want is you," he said, his voice an odd combination of whine and anger. "And it's not working, because you don't want me, no matter what I do."

He met her eyes, and she saw the spark of anger just waiting to ignite.

"It's not you, Ethan," she said, backing away. Her mind was whirring like a computer, making connections. *The typewriter.* He had access. *The photograph.* He could easily have gotten on her fire escape. The robbery. The women. All of it.

He was here the whole time. Watching, in the background, waiting. He'd seen Marina at the lectures. He could have easily been the pervert on her e-mail list.

Oh, God. *Oh, God.*

Her heart raced, blood pounding in her ears. She'd been right about Nat. And now her innocent brother was locked in a cell, and she was trapped in the break room with a psychopath. She stifled a whimper, wishing Jack were there to blow him away. But he was with the district attorney, preparing to testify at some trial, and Ronnie was all alone with a monster.

"I mean, I try so hard," he said, coming all the way around the table. "And with women, nothing. And then I try harder. And I do things for them." He looked at her with the icy calm of a killer. "Like for you. I've done a good job for you, right?"

She nodded, her hand fluttering near her throat. "Of course you have. Excellent." She took another step backward, then realized she was pressed up against the wall. *Shit.*

"I mean, I may be a little shy, but I'm trying to get better. All I want to do is be with someone, you know?"

Jack had checked Ethan out. How could this be happening? He seemed so normal.

So did Ted Bundy, a little voice said.

No. She was not going to die. She wanted Jack. She wanted children. And she damn sure wanted to live.

He reached out. Reached for her.

She screamed, every muscle in her body springing into action. She pushed him aside with a strength she didn't even know she possessed. He stumbled and she lunged for his toolbox, her hand closing around the wrench.

His eyes widened and he let out a horrible yell, rushing her, trying to take the wrench, trying to get to her. She swung blindly, throwing her entire body weight behind the heavy tool. It hit him square on the head. He stumbled. Blinked. His mouth opened into a curious little *O* as he started to fall.

Ronnie didn't wait for him to hit the ground.

She ran.

chapter
seventeen

Jack got to Ronnie's store from the district attorney's office in less than seven minutes. He screeched to a halt, blocking a lane of traffic, and left his door hanging open as he rushed inside.

He found her there, curled up in a plush chair, a female officer sitting with her and holding her hand. Ronnie looked up at him, the fear and weariness evaporating when she saw him, and his heart melted.

"Jack," she whispered, standing up and clinging to him. "Oh, Jack." Her voice cracked. "I didn't have the gun… There was a wrench… And I—"

"I know," he said, stroking her back. "Shh. It's okay now. You're safe. We've got him."

He kept his voice calm, cool. Inside, he was screaming. They'd checked Ethan out thoroughly. How the hell had they missed this?

She pushed away, looking up at him with red-rimmed eyes. "Nat," she said simply.

Jack grimaced, the idea of Nat going free sitting uneasily on his shoulders. He told himself it was simply because he'd colored his perception of Nat with false assumptions, but the truth was, he just didn't like the guy. For Ronnie's sake, he'd try to get past that.

"What will happen?" she asked.

"The D.A. will dismiss the charges. He'll be home soon, maybe as early as tomorrow."

"How could this have happened?" she asked. "The police, everyone, so certain he could do something like that. Something that…sick."

He stroked her hair, holding her close to him. "The evidence," he said. "It was too damning." And it was. What had happened—this bizarre mix of circumstance and misunderstanding—was a one-in-a-million shot.

She took a deep breath, her body shaking a little. Then she tilted her head back and met his eyes. "Nothing is what it seems, is it?" she asked.

"I love you," he said, squeezing her hand. "No matter what, you can depend on that."

During the week, Jack had been too busy in the Bleeker trial to do much investigating of Ethan. Donovan was on the case, though, trying to dig up more facts. The circumstances and the attack on Ronnie had been sufficient probable cause to arraign, and now Ethan was sitting in a cell in Rikers. The judge had set bail at five hundred thou', but Ethan hadn't been able to make it.

With Donovan working his tail off, they were sure to find enough evidence by the time the case went to trial. And if this damn Bleeker trial would ever end, Jack could get back to being an investigator instead of testifying like a performing puppet.

By some miracle he found a parking space near his building and pulled in. He killed the engine, then glanced at his watch. He was actually running early, and he said a silent thank-you. After a much too busy week, he was finally having a romantic dinner with Ronnie, and he wanted to catch a shower first. He was still in his suit jacket, but he loosened his tie as he walked into his building.

He was just starting up the stairs when he heard the door open behind him. He turned back, and there Nat stood. All six feet something of him filling the frame.

Jack tensed, his hand automatically resting on the butt of his gun. Nat's eyes glanced down, but then he looked Jack dead-on and smiled. A genuine smile. Like two buddies meeting at a baseball game.

"I wanted to talk with you," Nat said. "I hope you don't mind me stopping by."

"What's on your mind?" Jack asked, forcing himself to be polite.

"Ronnie," Nat said. "I'm a little afraid Ronnie feels awkward around me, like I blame her for you guys locking me up. I'm not mad at her. She's my sister, and I love her, and what happened doesn't change that. I want her to realize that, but I don't know how to tell her." He shrugged. "I guess I want your help."

Jack nodded, then cocked a head toward the stairs. "Come on up," he said. "I was going to shower and change before heading over to her place. We can talk up there."

Nat nodded and followed. He seemed a little tense, but Jack supposed that was normal under the circumstances. After all, only days before Jack had been spending all his waking energy looking for evidence to keep Nat locked up for life.

"I'm glad to hear you're not holding anything against Ronnie," he said, opening his door and ushering Nat in. "She believed in you the whole time."

Nat shook his head. "Like I said, I love Ron. That's not the only reason I came by, though."

"Oh?"

Nat shrugged. "I thought you and I got off to a bad start." He flashed an endearing grin. "I mean, even before you decided I was a killer, I think we rubbed each other the wrong way."

Jack wasn't about to deny that. "Understandable. I was interested in your sister. You're her big brother. Oldest story in the book." He met Nat's eyes. "I'm even more interested in your sister now," he said.

Nat nodded. "I know. Another reason I thought we should make peace. I figured we might be in-laws some day."

Jack laughed. "You're more perceptive than I realized," he said, thinking about the ring he'd been eyeing. Two more months and he'd have enough saved to buy it.

He pulled his tie all the way off. "Listen, I've got to get

out of this outfit." He gestured toward his war zone of a kitchen. "I ripped the cabinets down," he said. "But I think the glasses are in the green box. And there's definitely soda in the fridge." He headed toward the bathroom. "Make yourself at home while I grab a quick shower. I'm sweating like a pig in this damn suit."

He shut the door and turned on the water, letting it blast for its usual five minutes before the water heater kicked in. He placed his palms on the bathroom counter, staring at his own reflection. "He's making peace, Jack," he said. "Don't be an asshole."

He drew in a deep breath. Nat was saying all the right things, but the man still left a bad taste in Jack's mouth. It was important to Ronnie, though, so he'd suck it up and make nice.

He ran his fingers under the spray. Still cold. Damn. But that meant he had time to grab a beer and bring it back in the shower with him.

As his hands closed around the doorknob, he froze. He heard the beep of his answering machine in playback mode, and then Ronnie's voice floating toward him. "… extra clothes so you can stay over. I love you. I miss you. See you soon."

What the fuck?

He yanked open the door but didn't even have time to go for his gun. The bullet caught him dead-on in the chest, knocking him back against the door frame.

His chest exploded with agony, the pain seeping through him like something black and alive. And as he lost consciousness, he saw Nat holster a pistol and smile at the answering machine.

"I'm on my way, sweetheart," he said. "I'm on my way."

Ronnie stepped back, her gaze sweeping the entire table. Irish linen she'd brought back from a trip to Kilkenny, her grandmother's china, and two of the crystal wine goblets she'd bought from the actual factory in Waterford. She cocked her head, her gaze appraising, then leaned over and straightened the flatware at one of the place settings. Better.

She headed back into the kitchen and peeked into the oven. She'd spent the afternoon making lasagna, and it was bubbling nicely. A crisp salad was already in the fridge, and she had garlic bread on the counter, wrapped in foil and waiting to warm.

With a fingertip pressed against her lip, she tried to think if she'd forgotten anything. She wanted the meal to be perfect. Jack had been working his tail off, and this was going to be their first real date without threats and murders and other assorted bits of madness peering over their shoulders.

Earlier she'd poured some chardonnay into one of her everyday goblets, and now she took a sip, carrying the glass as she puttered in the living room, straightening up a bit, killing time until Jack arrived.

She glanced at the clock above the oven and scowled. According to it, it was nine-thirteen and he was forty-three minutes late. Forty-five if she went by her watch.

Either way, he was late. It irritated her a little, especially since they'd been planning this dinner for days. But she took another sip of wine and told herself not to be bitchy. Maybe traffic was terrible, even at ten at night. Or he got called in on a case. Or maybe he was just running late and she was being clingy and whiny.

Mentally chastising herself, she headed to the living room window, then raised the sash and climbed out onto the fire escape. The air was hot, overly humid, and her skin tingled from the shock of going from the brisk temperature in the apartment to the oppressive heat on the fire escape.

Even in the summer, though, she loved it out here, with the night sky overhead and the gentle buzz of her quiet neighborhood below. Now she took another sip of wine, letting the rhythm of the city envelop her. She turned and leaned her back against the railing, staring toward her bedroom window. An unexpected shiver racked her body, and she wondered if she'd ever be able to look at that window without imagining that terrible photograph and picturing Ethan crouched on the fire escape, a camera glued to his face.

She shivered, half wishing she hadn't come outside in the first place. But she didn't go back in. Instead she kept looking, feeling oddly drawn to the window.

Jack had helped her install a roll-down blind behind the curtains, but it was raised now, and she could see the sliver of light from where the two halves of her curtains didn't quite meet.

She hugged herself, her palms going up and down over her arms. *He'd* stood there. Ethan. Right outside her window. And he must have stood close, too. Her curtains weren't in the photograph at all, which meant that he'd had the lens pressed almost against the window.

Morbidly fascinated, she moved to the window, kneeling down behind the decorative ironwork just like he must have, then leaning on it, pretending she had a camera. She crept forward, drawn by some perverse need to know exactly what he'd done.

She winced as pain seared her arm, just above her elbow. Jumping back up, she cursed, pressing against the wound with the palm of her other hand. Damn, that smarted.

Looking down, she could see a long scratch illuminated in the glow from her window. Not deep, but enough to ooze blood. She bit her lip, eyeing the filthy iron bars and wondering if her tetanus booster was up to date. At the very least, she ought to put some alcohol on it.

She climbed back into the apartment. Jack still hadn't arrived, and that was beginning to worry her. Hoping she was just being paranoid, she grabbed her phone and dialed his cell number.

No answer.

For a second, she debated dialing his beeper, but she couldn't remember the number. Instead, she decided to clean up her arm. Then, if he still hadn't arrived, she'd give Donovan a call and see if he knew where Jack was.

In the bathroom, she grabbed a bottle of alcohol, a box of bandages and some cotton balls. She took her supplies into the bedroom and sat cross-legged on the bed while she cleaned the scratch, then bandaged it up nice and neat. Probably overkill, but it gave her something to do and kept her mind off thoughts of the perverted Peeping Tom.

She lay there trying to relax and not worry while she waited for Jack. Her mind drifted, and her gaze settled on the little brown patch on the ceiling. A smile touched her lips, and she imagined Jack in tight jeans and a T-shirt, a handsaw in one hand and a hammer in the other. Not a bad image. She'd definitely have to take him up on his offer to fix the ceiling and Nat's floor.

Still staring up, she tilted her head, curious. The patch seemed different. Not darker or bigger, but there was something else strange about it. Alarm bells clanked in her mind, and although she wondered if she wasn't just being silly, she stood on the bed and looked more closely at the spot.

Was that a hole?

A cold chill settled over her. With her heart thumping wildly, she climbed off the bed and grabbed the upholstered ottoman she kept next to the bedroom window. She dragged it to the bed, then lifted it up onto the mattress. The balance was precarious, but she managed to climb up and steady herself with her fingertips on the ceiling.

It *was* a hole. And not from water dripping. Fresh. Newly drilled.

And conveniently located on her brother's floor.

Oh, shit.

She clasped her hand over the scratch on her arm, the memories assaulting her. Nat's scratch. Exactly like hers. Nat had said he'd been hanging pictures. But there'd been no pictures in the apartment when Jack and Ronnie had gone to look at the floor. Just the one photograph of her that had been framed and hanging for years.

Oh, God. Jack had been right all along. Ethan was innocent. Her brother was the killer.

And he'd been watching her for days. Watching her sleep. Watching her change clothes. Watching her with Jack. Watching *everything*.

With a start, she lost her balance, tumbling off the ottoman onto the bed. A horrific thought occurred to her—was he watching her now?

She didn't stop to look, just raced toward the front door. She had no idea where she was going—she just knew she had to get out. Nat was home, and that was too close for comfort.

She was halfway across the living room when she heard the light knock at the door. *Jack*. Thank God. She flung the door open, then froze.

Nat stood right there, holding a single red rose.

"Nat," Ronnie said, hoping her voice sounded normal. "You startled me. I was expecting Jack."

"I hope you're not disappointed to get me instead," Nat said. The man standing there was her brother, and yet it wasn't. The voice was the same, the face the same. But somehow everything was different. As if he'd bought a Nat mask and tugged it on too tight.

She licked her lips. "Instead?"

A smile touched the mask. "He's not here. He must be late. Or perhaps he's not coming at all."

"No, no," she said. "He's definitely coming." She wanted him to get the message—Jack was coming. Jack had a gun. Jack would be pissed.

"Whatever you say, sweetheart." He stepped past her into the room.

"Hang out if you want," she said, moving into the doorway. "I need to go run an errand."

He took her by the elbow, urging her back into the room. "I thought you were waiting for Jack," he said.

Her stomach constricted. "Right. I am. I wanted to run down to the bakery. Fresh bread for dinner."

"We'll be fine with whatever you have," Nat said. He pulled her all the way in and shut the door. Then he locked her dead bolt and pocketed the key.

She swallowed. Her other dead-bolt key was on the key ring in her bedroom. And without that key, there was no getting through that door. In or out.

Was he going to kill her? The thought crashed through her brain, and her knees went weak. She had to get out of there. Had to get help. She just didn't know how.

"The table is lovely," he said.

"Thank you," she whispered. *Play along,* a little voice whispered. *Play along, and live.*

"I love it when you cook for me."

"Lasagna," she said. She was watching his face, his eyes. Trying to gauge his mood. But she couldn't. It didn't matter, though. All that mattered was getting away.

But how?

"We can have more dinners like this, sweetheart, now that all the barriers have been stripped away."

"Barriers?" she asked.

"The lies. The sneaking around. We can be together now. No more hiding." He stroked her face and she fought not to flinch. "My tributes to you will no longer be made in secret."

She licked her lips, understanding dawning. "Is that what the little gifts were? Tributes to me."

"Of course. I thought you would realize. Thought you'd know." He cocked his head. "But you're not as smart as me, McDonald. It doesn't matter. I love you, anyway." His eyes, keenly piercing, met hers. "Tell me you love me."

Cooperate, Ronnie. Cooperate and live.

"I love you," she said.

"It's better now," he said. "With me. The other men…" He trailed off, shaking his head.

A new fear thumped in her chest. "What?" she whispered, already afraid of the answer.

"They weren't right for you," he said. "You figured that out on your own with Burt. But the detective had you in his spell, I'm afraid. I don't blame you. You didn't realize. He seduced you, and you fell. That's how women are."

He stopped then, as if waiting for her to say something.

"Yes," she said, hoping it was the right thing to say. "That's right. I fell."

"It's those books you read." His face reflected both passion and revulsion. "You're purer than that, Ronnie. I thought you'd have more pride. Not like those other women. They looked up to you, but they could never be you."

She pressed her lips together, trying to keep from screaming.

"You were almost ruined like they were," Nat said. "*He* almost destroyed you. He took you with his cock. He took you from me and he wouldn't give you back. But don't worry. I saved you. I took care of the problem for you." He took a lock of her hair in his hand, letting it caress his palm.

She flinched but didn't move. "How?" she asked. She had to force the word out, and now she closed her eyes. A bone-deep terror clung to her, and she was certain she already knew the answer.

"Never you mind," he said. "But he won't be bothering you anymore. Not ever." He held his hands out, as if encouraging her to give him a hug. "Say 'thank you,' Ronnie. Thank your big brother for taking care of that problem for you."

Her mouth filled with saliva as her stomach lurched, vomit rising in her throat. She fought it, gagging, her hand pressed over her mouth. *He killed Jack.* The words repeated over and over in her head. *He killed Jack.* Jack was dead.

Was this really happening?

"Say 'thank you,'" he said.

Oh, yes. This was happening. Hell had come to the third floor.

She pulled in a breath. "Thank you," she said, her voice monotone.

"You're welcome," he said. He moved to sit at the table. And although he didn't say anything, she assumed she was supposed to serve him.

The situation was almost too surreal to believe. Like some subservient Stepford wife, she turned off the oven, then lifted the pan out, setting it on the hot plate on the counter. It was heavy and hot, and the opportunity seemed almost too good to pass up.

Right on his head. Surely he'd pass out.

But then he twisted in his chair, pulling a gun out from the pocket of his jacket. He laid it on the table, his hand resting lightly on it. "Serve me a large piece," he said.

Ronnie wanted to cry. She just wanted to curl up in a little ball and cry. But she wasn't going to. She was going to fight.

How, she didn't know. But in the end, she'd win.

They said little during dinner, for which she was grateful. That gave her time to think, and by the time they were almost done, she had an idea. Mentally, she crossed her fingers, then asked Nat to pass the lasagna.

She scooped out another large piece. Way more than she could eat, but eating wasn't part of her plan. With the square of noodles and sauce balanced on the spatula en route to her plate, Ronnie sneezed, managing at the same time to fling the lasagna into her lap.

She jumped up. "Oh! Oh, damn! Look at this mess." She dropped the lasagna on her plate and dabbed at the tomato sauce stain on her short linen skirt. "I love this skirt." She laid her napkin on the table and pushed back with the chair. "I've got to change," she said. She met his eyes and forced a smile. "I'll be right back."

She held her breath all the way into her bedroom, half afraid he'd grab her collar and tug her back, and half afraid he'd just shoot her. But she made it okay, and she closed the door behind her.

Her skirt really was soaked, but she didn't have time to worry with that now. Her keys were on her dresser and she grabbed them up, debating whether or not she could get the key in, the dead bolt unlocked, and the door open before a bullet found her back.

Probably not. Damn.

She picked up the phone to call the police but heard nothing. No dial tone. Just dead air. He'd either cut the line or had taken the phone off the hook. Either way, she was out of luck. And her cell phone was in her purse out there with him.

Even the gun Jack had given her was useless, tucked away in the table by her front door. Basically, she had no weapons and was cut off from the world.

She just had to go.

She shoved the keys into the shallow pocket of her skirt, then kicked off her shoes. Barefoot, she padded to the window. Would he hear the clatter of the fire escape ladder? She didn't know, and she desperately wished she'd put on some music and cranked up the volume.

Quietly, she slid the window up, then stepped out onto the fire escape. So far, so good.

As far as she knew, it had been years since the ladder had been dropped down to the third floor. She hoped it worked. If it didn't, she was about to jump four stories.

She fumbled for the release, and the ladder sprang free, surprising her as it shot down to the next level with an ear-splitting clatter. *Shit.*

Ronnie didn't waste any time worrying about the noise. She hiked her skirt up, tossed a leg over and grabbed the rickety ladder. The whole fire escape seemed to sway and groan, but she knew that had to be her imagination.

She held her breath and started down.

When her nose was about level with the platform, she saw a shadow pass in front of her living-room window. She froze. Had he heard? Did he know she'd left the bedroom?

The shadow moved on, and she breathed again. At least until she heard the steady pounding inside her apartment.

"Ronnie? *Ronnie?*"

He was at her bedroom, pounding on her door.

Move.

She scrambled down the ladder, reaching the third level just as his feet pounded on the grating above her. She stumbled onto the landing, cursing whoever designed the fire escape to have the ladders on alternate sides on the various levels.

She smacked the next ladder with her foot, and it clattered down into place. As she climbed on, he called out her name. She froze, looking up, and saw his eyes blazing down at her. Icy eyes. Cold and distant.

"Ronnie," he said, his voice calm. Reasonable. "Where are you going? Don't you know I'd never hurt you? *Could* never hurt you."

She didn't know that, didn't know it at all, and she ripped her gaze away, scrambling faster down the ladder, needing to get to the street. Needing to get there *now*.

"*Bitch.*" His low curse filtered down to her, and she

swallowed. This wasn't her brother, wasn't the man who'd protected her from the monsters under her bed. He *was* the monster under the bed.

The monster was descending, hurrying down the ladder toward Ronnie's level. *Faster.* She needed to go faster.

Two more levels, with Nat racing behind her. When she finally jumped the last four or so feet, he was just reaching the first-floor fire escape.

As soon as she touched ground, she ran, the little bits of gravel and other street junk cutting into her bare feet. She stuck her hand in her pocket, retrieving her keys, clutching them in her fist so that the keys poked out. Brass knuckles for the yuppie set.

Nat hit ground behind her, and she sucked in air. He was wearing shoes, had longer legs, could run faster. He was going to catch her, and when he did…

Her legs pumped harder, fear driving her on. A dozen keys on her key ring and she didn't own a damn car. Where the hell should she go? The subway? The police station? The bakery?

The bookstore.

She almost stopped, the thought was so brilliant, so obvious. *Joan had Nat's key.* If she could just get inside, she'd be safe. He couldn't get her. Not through the interior or the exterior door. She could lock the door, dial 911 and wait for the cops to rescue her from her brother.

She raced around the corner, calling out for help as she sped through the alley, ignoring the searing pain in her feet. She could hear him breathing hard behind her, his feet pounding on the pavement. He sounded close, so very close, and she pushed herself harder, not daring to look around.

As she rounded the next corner, taking her out to the main street by the store's front door, she tripped, pain shooting through her knee. She cried out, scrambling back to her feet as warm, sticky blood trickled down her leg.

The door. She had to get to the door.

Her leg throbbed, but she pressed on, driven by fear of the monster behind her.

She called out again, begging someone to help her. But there seemed to be no one around in the mostly business district at this time. She was all alone in the dark.

At the door, she fumbled for the keys, her hand shaking as she tried to get the door key into the lock.

Pound-pound-pound.

The footsteps got closer.

"Ronnie," he crooned, not even breathless. "It's me. It's Nat. Please stop. Let's talk."

She could barely draw breath, her lungs burned so much. She tried again to open the door, the keys slipping out of her hands onto the pavement.

Shit! No, please, no.

She dropped to the ground, scooped the keys up tightly, then forced the key in. She turned it, the lock springing free, and she pressed the door open. With a little gasp, she slid inside the building, then threw her weight back against the door, her breath coming in uneven spurts as she struggled to get the key back into the lock so she could secure the dead bolt.

There he was.

She screamed as Nat's face appeared at the glass. The door shifted as he tried to push it open. She screamed again, the sound tearing out of her throat, and she pressed hard against the door at the same time she turned the key.

Safe.

His fist crashed through the glass, sending shards all over the floor of the store as he reached for her.

She jumped back, racing to the other end of the store. *The alarm,* she thought, slipping behind a bookshelf and breathing deep. *He's tripped the alarm.*

Surely the police were on their way.

She needed to hide. To wait. They'd help her. They'd save her.

The little bell above the door jingled, and she held her breath, willing herself not to cry. He'd reached through and turned the key.

He was in the store.

"Ronnie, my angel. Please don't run." Soft and soothing, his voice seemed to come from all around her. "I love you. I've always loved you. I'd never hurt you. You're my treasure. Don't you know that?"

He was moving toward her, his voice getting slightly louder. With her back to the bookcase, she slipped around, trying to edge around the case and head back toward the front of the store. If she could just get back to the street without him realizing, maybe she could get away.

Silence.

She listened, but the only sound she heard was the

frantic beating of her heart. Could he hear it, too? Did he know where she was?—

A hand closed on her shoulder. She took a breath to scream, but another hand covered her mouth.

"Shh." A whisper in her ear. Gentle. Demanding. Was he going to kill her now?

She struggled vainly against his hold, but he pulled her back.

"It's Jack," the voice whispered, and her entire body sagged with relief. "Stay very, very still."

Walking hurt, breathing hurt, hell, *living* hurt. But it was a hell of a lot better now that Jack had found Ronnie. Now that he knew she was alive.

He signaled for her to get down. "Backup's coming," he mouthed.

They heard a soft rustle on the far side of the store. Their eyes met, hers wide.

"Crawl to the door," he said. "You've got a clear path. I'm going after him."

"Jack, no."

He squeezed her hand. "It'll be okay."

"He's got a gun." Barely a whisper, her voice was still sharp with fear.

Jack winced. "Yeah. I know." A high-caliber one, if the searing pain in his chest was any indication. "I'm wearing Kevlar." He pointed to the door. "Stay low and go."

She headed off, and he turned, moving as quietly as a cat toward the back of the store. His gun was drawn and ready, his senses hyperaware as he listened for Nat.

The bastard was going down tonight.

Slowly he moved through the store, chasing shadows, looking for a killer who knew the nooks and crannies of the shadowy bookstore a hell of a lot better than Jack.

A sharp crack rang out to his left, and Jack dropped to a crouch, his gun at the ready. Something hard and heavy hit him on the head, and he tumbled forward, the gun clattering out of his hand and sliding across the polished wood floor.

His vision filled with red, then turned gray as he hit the ground. He immediately rolled over, going for his ankle holster, but Nat's foot smashed onto his chest, bearing down on the bruise from where the earlier bullet had slammed into the vest.

"I thought I already killed you," Nat said. "No matter. We'll take care of it now."

Jack struggled, going for Nat's ankle, but the other man crunched his heel down. Jack heard the ribs break even as the pain shot through his body like fire.

Nat aimed the gun at Jack's face. "I could have shot you in the back of the head," Nat said. "But I wanted you to know I'd won. Wanted you to see me. To know Ronnie is mine."

"You can kill me," Jack said, struggling futilely under the pinion of Nat's leg. "But that won't make Ronnie yours."

An icy smile touched Nat's lips. "Stay away from my sister," he said, cocking the gun.

A shot rang out, and Nat stumbled backward, a red stain spreading across his white shirt. His eyes widened with surprise and pain, and a single word formed on his lips as he sagged to the floor—"Ronnie."

Ronnie slipped through the darkness to crouch at Jack's side, the gun still clutched in both hands. "It's over, Nat," she said. "You stay away from my boyfriend."

epilogue

The morning of the funeral was gray and dreary. Appropriate, Ronnie thought, as she walked hand in hand back to the limo with Jack.

The monster was dead.

Ronnie shivered despite Jack's arm around her shoulder. She wanted to remember the brother she'd loved, not the demon who'd been revealed. But it was all a tangled mess. *Time*, she thought. Maybe in time the hurt would go away.

"How are you doing?" Jack asked.

She nodded. "Still a little in shock, I guess. It comes and goes."

"It will get better," Jack said. "It's truly over now."

That it was. Her shot had pulverized Nat's shoulder, but it hadn't killed him, and once the hospital had discharged him, he'd confessed to everything—the notes, the murders, even the fake robbery to cover his tracks.

He'd pleaded insanity and taken a plea bargain. The day after his transfer to the institute, he'd ripped his hospital gown into strips, tied them together and hung himself.

"I still can't believe I never saw it," she said. "Never realized what he was. What he thought about me."

"He loved you," Jack said. "In his own twisted way, I think he really did. If you have to hold on to anything, just cling to that."

Ronnie nodded. "I know." The psychologist had told her his theory, which pretty much matched Jack's hypothesis. Nat had put her on a pedestal. He'd built her up into some perfect romantic vision of a lover. But he also wanted her. Passionately. And he was obsessed by the erotica she sold in the store. In his twisted mind, the notes he'd left the other women were his way of cleansing Ronnie. Of proving that she was more pure than the others.

There were still open questions. Some they might never answer. Nat had lied about having an affair with Marina, but Jack believed he'd watched her and stolen her keys. As for Caroline, they really had been having an online affair, and the police believed he'd arranged to meet her in person, probably more than once. And then he'd killed her to cover up the evidence.

She shook her head, remembering how it had all come down. "Poor Ethan," she said. "He was just trying to practice being assertive, and I took him down." She met Jack's eyes. "I feel like I attacked the Maytag repairman."

Jack laughed softly. "Considering all the business you've referred his way, I think you've made it up to him."

Ronnie nodded. "And I even gave him a few more

jobs at the store. Basically anything I could think of that sounded remotely electrical."

Jack laughed. "I'm glad you're not selling the store," he said.

"Me, too," Ronnie admitted. She'd thought about it, but decided that would be like giving in. Nat had always wanted her to—apparently so she'd have the money and time to travel with him and so she'd be clean of the erotica "filth." Plus, she didn't want to lose the memories of her father.

But she could never live in the apartment again. And as soon as she could find a real estate agent, she was going to list them for sale. But not the store below.

"You're sure you want me living with you?" she teased. "You're a big-shot homicide detective now."

Jack laughed. He'd switched divisions soon after the case had closed, and when she'd asked him about it, he'd simply said that he could now. She hadn't pressed, but she'd been happy to know that whatever demons he'd been battling were dead now. Maybe that had been Nat's legacy. One tiny bit of good from the horror.

"We big-shot detectives are allowed to share our apartments," he said. "And our beds."

Ronnie shook her head, biting back a grin. "I don't know. Your apartment's pretty small. Tight quarters." She trailed her finger down his arm. "We'll be right on top of each other. Are you sure?"

He kissed her hand, holding on to her fingers. "Very sure." Then he reached into his pocket and pulled out a small velvet box. "In fact, I'd like you to live there permanently."

Her heart skipped a beat as she eyed the box, then looked at Jack's face. She saw love shining there, and Ronnie knew that with Jack at her side she could get through anything. "Yes," she said. "Oh, yes."

He opened the box and slipped the most beautiful platinum solitaire onto her finger. A tear spilled down her cheek, and she leaned in for his kiss.

"I love you," she said.

"I know, sweetheart. I love you, too."

And right then, Ronnie thought, that was all that mattered.

* * * * *